About the author

Jamie Burn grew up in Newcastle Upon Tyne. He was awarded a first in Philosophy at Sheffield University and a Masters with distinction in Policy Studies at Edinburgh University before joining London-based think tank Policy Exchange. He went on to work in the biotechnology industry as a policy officer.

The Little Boy with his Head in the Clouds is based on his memories of weekends with his grand-parents in the Tees Valley.

THE LITTLE BOY WITH HIS HEAD IN THE CLOUDS

A Children's Story

Jamie Burn

Book Guild Publishing

First published in Great Britain in 2015 by
The Book Guild Ltd
9 Priory Business Park
Wistow Road
Kibworth
Leics LE8 0RX

Typesetting in Century Schoolbook by
Nat-Type, Cheshire

Printed in Great Britain by
CPI Group (UK) Ltd, Croydon, CR0 4YY

A catalogue record for this book is available from
The British Library.

ISBN 978 1 910508 26 8

Contents

1

Golden Boy

Have you ever wondered what normal means? Does normal mean like you or me? Is normal how we're meant to be? Well, this is the story of a little boy who wasn't normal at all.

He lived in a very ordinary little house with windows, a front door, a roof and four walls. It had a neat and tidy little garden at the back with a well-mown lawn and pretty flower beds. Inside it was snug, which is to say really quite small, but it had a big fireplace in the living room for burning wood.

And in this house a normal family lived. You could see whether they were in by the smoke that billowed from the chimney pot.

As you would expect, this little boy's mum and dad loved him very much.

They called him 'Golden Boy' because his thick blond hair gave him a halo like an angel's. But his real name was Burt Marshmallow and he certainly wasn't a saint.

Burt had a big sister whom he nicknamed 'Pigtails'. He felt she picked on him all the time.

And she told tales when he was naughty. They

fought a lot, as brothers and sisters often do, but they would have been very lonely if they didn't have each other to talk to.

Burt's ordinary life didn't stop him having extraordinary adventures. You see, Burt found normal life rather boring and he thought that there was nothing worse in the whole wide world than being bored.

What Burt really wanted to do was to play and have fun all of the time. But then when he was having fun, his mum or dad or Pigtails would interrupt. They would say: 'Stop doing that, Burt; it's naughty. And tidy up that mess, for goodness' sake.'

Burt didn't like being told what to do at all. In fact, Burt thought, if there was anything worse than being bored, it was being told what to do when you didn't want to do it.

Burt's biggest problem was that his ordinary little house was directly, smack bang in the middle of nowhere. So he had no friends to play with. Now don't get me wrong, it wasn't all bad. Burt's house was surrounded by mountains and rivers and meadows, and by woodland where the trees grow. And Burt spent most of his time playing outside with his dog, Sandy.

Sandy was a golden retriever and she had been trained as a guide dog. Guide dogs are funny dogs because you don't walk them, they walk you. They're trained to help people who can't see for themselves. Burt thought that Sandy was probably cleverer than most people. And Burt would know because he always knew exactly what she was thinking. They were best friends and they had lots of games they liked to play together, like chasing the cat, or hide and seek, or playing pretend, which was a game that Burt called 'make-believe'.

Make-believe is where you imagine a magical place full of special people and the exciting things that happen to them. Most importantly of all, you pretend that you are in the story, and that the exciting things are really happening. This was Burt's favourite game because it was always different, although Sandy preferred chasing the cat.

Now, most adults thought Burt was a funny little boy. He had what they called an 'overactive imagination'. Personally, I'm not at all certain that you can be too imaginative. That would be like being too clever, or too funny, neither of which are a problem at all. But everything does have a time and a place, and Burt seemed to spend all of his time in another place, pretending to be someone else entirely.

As Burt got better at imagining, he discovered he could do fun things even when he was asleep. He would dream all night long about being a brave warrior in a magical land, where he fought monsters of all shapes and sizes.

He would just make up his own stories out of thin air in his head. And he liked dreaming so much that he would keep on dreaming in the day. In daydreams you can do anything.

In his favourite dream, Burt was a knight. He

was brave Sir Burt and Sandy was his trusty horse. He would build a castle in his head, which he would use as a base for fighting monsters. And they would go on imaginary adventures. Burt did most of the fighting himself with a sword and a shield, wearing armour to protect him. But Sandy also helped, and – do you know? – they beat the monsters every time.

Burt got to be so good at make-believe that he could pretend to be anything at all, like a wizard transforming himself...

On his bike Burt became a swooping bird
So fast he could take off and fly
Though he wasn't good at landing
So it hurt and made him cry

And if somebody gave him a present
He'd give them a big sloppy kiss
But the box would soon be a castle
And he'd give the toy a miss

At a pool he'd go and jump straight in
Forgetting he couldn't swim
Like a fish he'd try to dive deep down
Til his dad came to rescue him

Burt was a bit of a wild child and people found him very curious indeed.

They would say things like, 'He's away with the fairies that lad' and 'That boy's got his head in the clouds.'

4

2

Burt's Family Tree

Every day in the evening Burt would walk Sandy with his dad. He would hold the lead in one hand and his daddy's hand in the other, and they would talk all the way to the nearest village and back.

Burt's dad was a gardener, the head gardener for a rich family. He used to be a farmer but the rich family bought his land and now he worked for them, planting pretty plants. His dad knew everything there was to know about plants and animals and the natural world.

And he taught Burt on their walks. He would point to things and say what they were and Burt would collect them in his 'interesting things' box.

One autumn before the school year began Burt was collecting fallen leaves from different trees that had turned lots of lovely colours. He collected conkers to put on a string and to take to his school for conker fights! His dad told him that conkers were special seeds and if you let them grow they would turn into trees!

They would search for presents for his mum together, like flowers and precious stones. Burt would draw pictures and make collages because presents made her happy, and that made Burt feel good as well. Plus, his dad said, presents got you brownie points and he spent his in the village pub.

Some days Burt's dad asked what he wanted to be, and Burt would reply something different each time. Once he said: 'I want to be a lion I think, so I can eat all the people who are nasty to me.'

'Well, you know, people are only nasty to you if you're naughty to them,' his daddy explained. 'Like when you chased the cat with a broom and she hissed and scratched you and you complained.'

After a while they came to a wishing well, which lay just off the track. It was made of carved stone that was very worn down and if you looked in the water it was full of treasure.

Burt's dad gave him a coin to throw in. He said: 'You can make a wish or spend it on sweets.'

Burt threw it in and made a wish.

His dad said, 'Just be careful you don't wish your life away.'

So instead of wishing to be a lion, a bird or a fish, Burt wished he knew everything like his dad. That wish would come true because every day he always learned something new.

They walked on and saw a rainbow in the hills and his dad said: 'Did you know that rainbows are made out of sunlight? It bounces off the raindrops and the light breaks open. And inside are all the pretty colours that shine down from the sun. Everyone sees their own rainbow: each rainbow is different for everyone.'

6

Burt had read a little about rainbows. 'Is it true that there's treasure buried at the end of a rainbow?'

His dad just laughed and said, 'Maybe!' so Burt ran off and tried to catch it, but it kept on getting further away.

'You never know, you might find it one day, my lad.'

When they got back his dad collapsed in a chair and Burt helped his mum serve up the dinner. Then he helped her do the washing, which she did even though she had a job too, as a cleaner at the rich people's house.

'I wish your dad would help more like you,' she said. 'I hope you don't grow into a lazy old man.'

Burt enjoyed helping her because, instead of telling him things, his mum asked him lots of questions and he told her everything he knew.

'Why do socks always go missing in the wash, Burt? I keep buying pairs and then one gets lost.'

Burt thought about this for a while and investigated the funny machine she used. Eventually he said, 'I think this is a space rocket. Maybe aliens from Mars are collecting odd socks.'

One summer Burt's dad took him to see something special. They walked through the meadows for miles and miles until they came to an old oak tree that stood at the end of a field. It had branches that sprawled out like great muscly arms and big roots that stuck out of the ground like legs sitting in a sandpit.

'This is our family tree,' his dad said. 'Do you know what a family tree is?'

'No,' Burt admitted. Then he thought about it. 'But you and Mummy and Pigtails are my family. Did you come out of this tree?'

'Not exactly,' his dad chuckled. 'You're right about us being a family, but actually our family is much bigger. Because myself and your mum had parents and brothers and sisters and they are your grandparents and uncles and aunts. And the parents of your grandparents are your great-grandparents, and your aunt and uncle's children are your cousins. If you write down your whole family – all the children who grew up and had children of their own – and you draw lines to join them up, it looks just like the branches of a great big tree. And that, my boy, is a family tree.'

'Oh,' said Burt thoughtfully.

'But our family tree is much more special than most,' his dad continued, 'because it really grew out of the ground. Your great, great-granddad planted this tree as a sapling when he went to a war in a distant land. It was a baby tree he uprooted from the woods nearby and he carried it to this spot, which used to be the farm our family owned. And before he left he told your great-granddad that he had left his spirit behind in this tree. He said it would look after him, so that he could look after the rest of the family, and he told him to come here to remember him and ask his advice if he didn't return ...'

'You can talk to trees?' Burt interrupted.

'Of course, they're very good listeners.'

'Your great, great-granddad was killed in that war, and he fought so bravely he was given a special medal. But you see, he fought so bravely because he knew he couldn't really die. His spirit lived on in his family tree, and this tree still keeps an eye on us. Your great-granddad and granddad before me proposed to their wives in this spot, and this is where I came to ask your mum to marry me. And when I was little I used to climb up to the top. I even built a tree house up there with my dad … Can you see?'

With that his dad lifted Burt up on to one of the branches. Burt felt funny and unsteady being so high up at first, but his dad was there to catch him, so he started to shuffle around and he even stood up carefully. And up there in the branches he could see his dad's old tree house. It was a wooden box, with a hole for a door and another for a window. It looked a bit like the boxes he had seen birds living in. There was a frayed piece of rope that had snapped so that the ends dangled below.

The whole thing looked twisted and rickety, like the tree had hugged it too tightly and squished it.

'What's a tree house for?' Burt asked staring with wonder.

'A tree house is your very own place where you can sit and think and look out at the world. You can hide special things there, and you can take all your friends there. I tried to bring your mother here once, but she was too scared to climb up.' His eyes seemed to twinkle with a smile as he said this.

9

'Can I play in the tree house now?' Burt asked. His dad shook his head.

I'm sorry, son, but it's not safe anymore. The tree has broken it, you see, and it's grown too high for us to climb up to. Perhaps when you get a bit older, you can build a tree house of your own. Anyway, we're a long way from home – we'd best get back. C'mon, let's go.'

And off they went, with Burt sitting on his dad's shoulders. As he was carried along, Burt imagined he was a big, tall grown-up.

3

Burt's Big Idea

One day Burt and Sandy were in the garden playing a game called detectives. They were the police and they hunted for baddies. Sandy was snuffling and sniffing for clues.

This was fun for a while but Burt was getting that bored feeling. They had investigated this garden many times and there weren't really any baddies to fight, except Pigtails. It was clear that they needed something to do.

Then Burt had a brainwave. It hit him like a bucket of water being thrown in his face. He jumped up and hopped around excitedly and Sandy bounded over barking, because she always got excited when Burt did.

Burt stopped and calmed himself.

'We are going to build our very own tree house, Sandy, which we will use as a base for fighting baddies. We'll keep all of our things there, so Pigtails can't steal them, and we can even invite our friends from school there and we'll have a club, like an army for fighting monsters. I'll be the leader and you can be my deputy!'

Well, this was all very exciting, and Sandy could barely contain herself. She started rolling on the ground and rubbing her back on the grass while Burt tickled her. But then she hopped up and barked: *Woof!* And Burt knew exactly what she meant. They didn't have a tree.

Then Burt had another idea! He went and fetched a conker from his room. Then he went over to the flowerbed and scraped out a hole. He had remembered that conkers grow into trees!

He placed the conker carefully in the hole, leaving the light brown circle looking up. Then he covered it up and sat down cross-legged. And he crossed his arms and his fingers and he waited.

But nothing happened.

Sandy had a wee on it for good measure, and Burt remembered it needed rain. So he went and got the watering can, and he gave it some water, which, he thought, it probably preferred to Sandy's wee. But nothing happened all day long.

That evening he sat and had dinner and told his mum and dad about his plan. To his surprise, they both laughed at him.

'You can't grow a tree overnight, my boy,' his dad chuckled. 'I told you, you'll have to wait until you're old enough and then we'll fix up my old tree house together. How's that?'

Well Burt didn't say anything. But after his dinner he went up to his room and looked out the window, which was something he did when he was thinking hard. Then he felt a bit tired so he plonked himself face down on his bed.

He didn't like the idea of 'when you're older'. In fact, he didn't like waiting at all. Waiting was one of those things that made him bored and, as I've said, Burt hated being bored. *And* he didn't like being told he couldn't have a tree house. He didn't like being laughed at, not one little bit. The more he thought about it, the more he thought he didn't want his dad's old tree house. He wanted his very own secret place that no one else knew about. He lay like that and sulked all night, until he fell asleep with all his clothes on.

That night Burt had a dream. It was about a girl who lived underwater. Now Burt didn't usually like girls but that was just him being silly and this girl seemed very nice, and she spoke in an echoey, underwatery voice. And she told him ... something.

Well, he couldn't remember exactly what she told him. He had woken up and he was sweating even though the window was wide open. What had the girl said, he wondered as he got undressed. He fell back to sleep thinking about it.

Then he had another dream. This time he dreamt about a colossal, gigantic, enormous tree. It was the tallest tree in the woods nearby and he climbed to the top and felt the breeze on his face and he could see for miles and miles. It was so high, he could even see the clouds drifting by. Then magically some planks of wood appeared and he held a hammer in one hand and nails in the other for making a tree house. But Burt couldn't seem to hit them into the wood. They kept bending, or he hit his finger, or he fumbled and dropped them.

Then as one got away he tried to catch it and he ...
FELL!

Burt woke up as if he had landed on his bed and
bounced back up again. He leapt up and got
tangled in his covers and fell on to the ground. He
couldn't work out where he was or what had
happened, and he was breathing hard as though
he had just run a race at the school sports day.

Burt's mum poked her head around the door.
She was going to say something, then she saw him
there on the floor and looked concerned.

'Did you have a nightmare, my love?'

'No, I wasn't scared. It was a happy dream but I
couldn't do what I wanted and in the end I fell out
of the tree.'

'Ah well. Maybe something's trying to tell you
not to build a tree house.' His mum smiled a big
wide smile. How had she known what his dream
was about?

'Can I walk Sandy after breakfast?' he asked.

'Of course you can, but don't go too far and make
sure you wait with Sandy when you're crossing the
road. That dog's so clever I think she could walk
herself.'

She said this as she was tugging Burt's pyjamas
over his head, and getting his clothes out of the
drawer and combing his hair. She always seemed
to be doing two things at once, and for a while Burt
was distracted by trying to decide who was
cleverer – Mummy or Daddy. Then he thought
about the girl in his dream again. She would turn
into a mummy. And he would turn into a daddy.

And he wondered if you could dream up real people.

After his breakfast of smiley-faced eggs, to which his dad had added tomato sauce for the mouth and eyes, Burt set out with Sandy.

'You wouldn't want to walk yourself, would you?' he asked Sandy.

Sandy wagged her tail and tugged him along because she thought she was walking him.

Eventually they got to where Burt wanted to go, which was the wishing well. Burt dug in his pocket and pulled out, not a coin, but another conker. He threw it in and looked at his face as it rippled in the water. Then he scrunched up his eyes and he made a wish.

'Can you make my conker turn into a tree? I wish I had a giant tree of my own that reached right up into the clouds, with lots of strong branches for climbing up and for building a big tree house on, like my very own castle. I would have real adventures and fight real monsters and I could make lots of friends to play with … Can you make that happen for me?'

Burt went home and checked his conker in the garden, but it was still hiding underground. He checked it everyday for the next week but still nothing grew. By the time the school holidays came Burt had decided he would have to dream up something else if he was ever going to get his tree house.

4

The Ghost in the Garden

In the school holidays Burt found himself alone and bored an awful lot of the time. Then one night he dreamt about a monster that lived under his bed. It climbed up the bed covers and into his head and it gave him his first real nightmare.

It was a scaly, slimy one-eyed monster with big sharp teeth and claws and it smelt like vegetables.

In a horrible snarly voice it told Burt it was going to get him. Then it chased him and, try as he might, Burt couldn't escape.

The monster was chasing him and it said he had to play with it or it would gobble him up, and Burt was so scared he stumbled and fell and he was sliding backwards on his bottom into a corner. Then it pounced and Burt woke up and he threw off the covers and stood up. *It must have crawled back under the bed*, he thought.

'It's OK, it's OK,' he told himself. He was trembling all over. It was dark and the room was full of scary shadows, and he listened as hard as he could while his eyes adjusted to the light. He

16

thought he could hear the monster moving around and growling underneath him.

Well, most little boys would have called for their mum and dad, but Burt remembered his wish. He might not have his tree house yet, but here was a real live monster for him to fight and that meant he had his very own adventure.

Burt found that thinking these brave thoughts instead of thinking about how scared he was made him feel less afraid. In fact, it made him feel quite as brave as he wanted to be. So he stood there on the bed and plucked up his courage, and as he made up his mind his legs stopped shaking and his face took on a determined scowl, like a superhero. Then he said in his most booming voice:

'You are horrible and I don't *want* to play with you! Get out from under my bed or I'll come and biff you on the head.'

Then he leapt down and spun around in a flash, ready to doof the monster up, but it had vanished into thin air – PUFF. He must've scared it away.

'Ha-ha!' Burt cried, victorious, and he jumped back on to his bed and jumped up and down on the mattress singing 'I'm the king of the castle, and you're the dirty rascal.' And he knew then and there that the monster would never dare return.

His mum and dad, of course, came rushing in. Dad was quite angry that he was causing a racket so late. Burt told them all about his fight with the monster, and he might have exaggerated a little but they didn't believe him. His mum just shushed him and his dad told him to stop being silly. Burt was upset by this. He hated it when grown-ups ignored him and didn't take him seriously.

The next day, in the garden, Burt told Sandy all about his fight with the monster and how it had run away when he had shouted at it, and Sandy believed him. She thought they should track down the monster so that it couldn't scare any other children. Burt was considering this when something strange happened. A breeze seemed to blow through the garden, making Burt feel chilly. The back gate swung open with a squeak and a crack.

Burt was looking around because he had a funny feeling he hadn't felt before. And Sandy started barking at thin air. Then, right in front of him, a ghost appeared, looking straight down at him. It looked like the shadow of someone he knew; it looked exactly like a shadow standing up.

Just like a person in a dream, Burt had trouble making out its face at first. He could see it wasn't a scary ghost. In fact, it was wearing a happy grin and its eyes looked like the eyes of someone who was daydreaming. Finally, when Sandy stopped barking and instead made a low grumbling growl, the ghost spoke.

'Hello, little boy. Don't be afraid. My name is Ghastly the ghost. What's yours?'

'My name is Burt Marshmallow and this is my dog Sandy ... Sshhhh,' he said to Sandy, though she kept on growling.

'I've been watching you. You look awfully bored.'

'No, I'm fine,' said Burt. 'I fought my first real

monster last night and we're trying to decide where it might have run away to.'

'Well, you sound like a very brave little boy, and you're very friendly, too. I wonder if you can help me. I'm lost, you see. I'm looking for the woods nearby. Do you know the way?'

Burt gasped. 'Why are you going to the woods? Do you have a tree house there?'

The ghost's eyes lit up. 'Why yes! Do you like tree houses? Would you like to come and play in mine?'

'Well ...' Burt was unsure about this. He knew he wasn't supposed to talk to strangers. 'Why are you in my garden?' he asked at last.

'I'm looking for an adventure, that's all. I want to go and play in the woods, and I need someone to play with. But if you're too scared, that's OK. I'll go and find somebody braver.'

'No wait, what games are you going to play?'

'Oh I don't know. Hide and Seek is my favourite. But I like Stuck-in-the-Mud and What's the Time, Mr Wolf? and Wild Goose Chase, which is a bit like tig. Do you know them?'

Burt couldn't decide whether he trusted this ghost entirely, even if it did look familiar somehow. Ghastly wasn't a very nice name, so its mummy and daddy couldn't have liked it very much. And it had a funny look in its eye now that reminded him of the monster in his dream, like it was frightened, excited and hungry all at once. And it kept staring at him, although when he looked it in the eye, it looked away, as if it was hiding something.

Burt was very suspicious. Sandy didn't seem to

like Ghastly at all and she was a good judge of character, so his dad always said. He was about to make his excuses and go inside when a thought occurred to him.

'If you're lost, how are you going to find the woods?'

'I have a friend who lives nearby called Flutterby. She's a fairy. She'll know how to get us there.'

Well, Burt wasn't sure about this ghost but a fairy sounded nice and helpful. And he couldn't help thinking about finding his tree.

'I'm going to take my dog for a walk. I'd like to know where the woods are as well so I can find my very own tree and build a tree house to live in. But I'm afraid you can't come; I'm not allowed to go off with strangers.'

'Very well,' said the ghost, looking a little bit miffed. 'I'll just have to set the monster on you.' Ghastly glared at Burt with its cold, dead eyes. It was clearly planning a nasty surprise.

'I am the ghost of everything bad. I feed off happiness and make children feel sad. Then they become like me, all lost and alone.

'I steal their souls where the happy thoughts go, and in its place I leave my ghastly shadow to scare them witless until they do as I say. I give children nightmares that keep them awake at night and I know the monster that scares you.

'So you must do exactly as I say or I'll tell everyone you've become a monster as well.'

Burt was scared, but he didn't show it. 'Actually

I chased the monster away and I have dreams, not nightmares. I dream good things up all night and all day. So it's going to take more than you to scare me. You look as though you're already dead and you smell like a rubbish bin, full of rotting old food.'

The ghost looked puzzled and a little bit frightened. 'You're just a little boy. You must do as you are told. And what do you mean I smell?!'

Burt ignored this. He stuck out his chest and boomed: 'I am Burt Marshmallow and I don't have to do anything you tell me. And if you're not careful, my dog Sandy will get you.'

Woof! Sandy agreed.

Ghastly squealed like he had just seen a mouse or turned into one. Almost at once, however, he recovered. 'You'd better back off or I'll go get my dog Wolf.'

Burt felt like a superhero. He wasn't scared of this ghost at all. 'That's OK, we'll go and get him, just as soon as we've taken care of this monster of yours. And why do you do what he says?'

Ghastly couldn't believe his ears. It tried to disappear but it was trapped by Burt's glare. It had never met a little boy this brave before and it didn't like it one little bit. And what was worse, there was something in Burt's eyes that made it feel worse than it had ever felt. Burt was making the ghost feel like it wasn't scary at all and that made it feel horrible.

'I was only kidding, honestly,' it snivelled at last. 'Please don't tell people I'm bad. It's the nasty monster who did this to me. It lives in a house in the woods over there ...' The ghost pointed into the distance. '... by the enchanted river in Wood-Land. I promise I won't haunt anyone else if you get the monster and set me free. You can find it and I'll leave you alone. You just need to follow the stream.'

Burt felt funny. He felt stronger than he had ever felt and don't ask me why but a magic grew inside him. He had discovered that he had a magic stare that could root out all evil and show it to people. And he knew he had an inner strength that this ghost could not defeat.

When Burt looked the ghost in the eye, it couldn't escape his judgement. And even though Ghastly was bigger than him, he felt as if he was looking down on it. And do you know, it started to shrink away like a shadow at midday, and its voice grew more and more squeaky and high-pitched, like it was sucking the air out of a floating balloon.

'Wait, what are you doing? I don't like it. Stop looking at me. Don't look at me. No, no, go away pleeeeeeaaaase.'

Burt didn't feel sorry for the ghost at all. It shouldn't be on the monster's side.

The ghost was smaller than Burt by now and it started to shake and tremble before his magic eyes. They shone through its shadow figure like a torch in the night and it began to fade and disappear from view entirely.

Then Burt shouted at the top of his lungs:

'YOU ARE HORRIBLE AND I DON'T WANT TO PLAY WITH YOU!'

Then he turned his back on it and, like a burst balloon, the ghost went POP, BANG, WHIZ, FLOP, and disappeared into thin air.

Burt and Sandy looked at each other. 'That was easy!'

Woof! Sandy agreed. Then she went and fetched her lead and Burt understood – it was time for walkies.

Sandy liked going for walkies so much, she forgot all about the ghost. She bounced up and down and crouched and spun and rolled around, while Burt fetched her some treats.

As an afterthought Burt ran into his room and took out his favourite toy: a catapult! Then they went down the garden path. This must be his wish coming true at last.

'Let's go and get all the baddies!'

5

The Church on the Hill

They walked off down the road in the direction the ghost had pointed. Burt had never been this way before. They came to a fence that led to a field full of sheep. The sheep looked at them and baa'ed, then they all hurried away together in a flock, which reminded Burt of a big cloud being blown around by the wind.

Then a farmer appeared whistling to his dog and his dog ran rings around the sheep, chasing them this way and that and keeping them all together. They were herded into a pen made out of wood and wire. Then the farmer closed the gate behind them and two young men sitting inside ambushed them. They grabbed them by the legs, turned them upside down and started giving them a haircut with giant scissors.

Burt shuddered. He hated getting his hair cut and they were being very rough.

Then the farmer looked at them and shouted.

'Oi, who are you? What are you doing in my field? That dog of yours frightened my sheep!'

Burt thought that was funny. They looked

frightened enough of the farmer's dog and those big horrid hairdressers.

'Why are you giving them a haircut?' he asked.

'Because we're shearing them, that's why, nosey parker! But never mind that. I should give you a clip round the lug for trespassing on my property! You don't see me nosing around in your garden, do you?'

Burt decided to ignore this. 'What does shearing mean?'

'It means we're giving them a haircut,' the farmer said, exasperated. 'They don't need their wool, now that it's getting warm, so I cut it off and sell it to old ladies. Then they can knit scarves and hats and woolly jumpers for their grandchildren at Christmas. And that keeps them warm in the winter and the sheep have grown more wool by then.'

'Oh,' said Burt. 'Can I pass through your field, please?'

'You most certainly cannot. Not with that dog at any rate. And anyway, where are you going? Where are your parents? Do they know you're out on your own?'

'Yes, they do.' Then he looked up and saw a funny-shaped house on a hill. It had a big tall tower and a bell was ringing noisily. It must be a doorbell, he thought, because people were going inside.

'I've just come down here to play with my dog. My daddy lives up there in that big tall tower.'

The farmer looked over his shoulder. 'That tower

is a spire, and that house is a church, my lad. Only God lives in there, unless your father is the vicar.'

'Yes, that's what I meant,' Burt said, fibbing a bit. He didn't really understand what the farmer had said.

He had once heard his daddy say, 'What in God's name are you doing, Burt?' And when Burt had asked who God was, he'd been told he was like Santa Claus. 'He answers wishes called prayers, but only if you're good.' Burt had assumed God lived in Lapland with Santa. Why hadn't his dad told him he lived this close by?

Anyway, the farmer looked quite impressed all of a sudden. 'Oh well, why didn't you say? How is your father the vicar? You give him my regards. Get on your way and tell him I'll see him on Christmas Day.'

'I will,' said Burt. 'Thank you kindly.' And off he went up the hill.

Burt let Sandy off her lead and they ran to the top chasing sticks until they reached a stone wall and another gate. On the other side there were lots of old stones in the ground, like rows of teeth in a giant mouth, and the church stood in the middle like a big tongue sticking out at the sky.

They set off towards the church, stepping over funny mounds and piles of flowers. Some of the stones were covered in names and dates and others were covered in moss. Then as he stood there reading one a witch appeared at the gate. She had a hunched back and a big stick and was dressed entirely in black.

'Do you know what this stick is for?' she cackled, waving it in the air and pointing at him? Burt shook his head. It didn't look like a broomstick.

'It's for little boys who go dancing on people's graves,' she said.

'I'm not dancing,' Burt said, a little confused.

'Well, what on earth are you doing on there?' she demanded. 'That's my Arthur's grave.'

Burt looked down. He was standing on a mound in front of a shiny new gravestone.

'I'm terribly sorry,' he said. 'What's a grave? And who is Arthur?'

'Arthur was my husband and that is his grave. Don't they teach you anything in Sunday school these days?'

'I don't go to school on a Sunday,' Burt replied. 'And I didn't know witches had husbands. Do you have little witchlings as well?'

'How dare you call me a witch, you cheeky little blighter! I did have children and if I was half the woman I was then I'd give you the spanking of a lifetime. Knock that cheek right out of you. Witch indeed, and standing on graves. No respect for the living or the dead, I say. I don't know – young people these days.'

She waved her stick at him and shooed him away.

'Clear off. Are your mummy and daddy in church already? I'll have a word with them, leaving you to run wild outside.'

Burt realised his mistake too late. This wasn't a witch at all. It was someone's grandmother dressed in black, and she was going to visit God as well.

'I'm sorry for calling you a witch and I'm sorry for standing on Arthur's grave. Only I don't know what a grave is, and I still won't unless you tell me.'

'Well, I don't know, you're a funny little boy. A grave is when people get old and tired of living in the world. When they're finished with their life they die and we put them to bed underground. Then where their soul goes nobody knows. The vicar will tell you it goes to God in heaven.'

'What's a soul?'

'The vicar told me a soul is who you really are inside, something you keep a copy of in your mind where you think ... But if you ask me, you're thinking too much and asking too many questions for your own good.'

Well, Burt knew there was no such thing as too many questions. How else was he supposed to learn everything and get his wish? And wasn't God supposed to answer wishes?

The old lady wandered off along the path, so he ran towards the church to find God. Maybe he would help him get the monster.

He came to a giant door and an old man with a grey beard was standing guard. He wore a black dress a bit like the old lady but Burt knew better than to call him a wizard. He went over and introduced himself.

'Hello, my name is Burt Marshmallow and this

is my dog Sandy. I've come to see God – the old man who lives inside. Is it you?'

'Hello, my child,' said the vicar. 'I'm the vicar, and this is my church. You've come to the right place to learn about God.'

'I'm not your child, that's just what I told the farmer. Does God work for Santa making presents for Christmas?'

'No, they don't know each other as far as I'm aware, but if anything Santa works for God. I'm afraid you're mistaken if you think you can meet God. You just have to take my word for what He says. I suppose you could say I'm one of His elves.'

'Well, I have some questions for God. Is he in there or not?'

'I'm afraid it's not that simple. God lives in the kingdom of heaven. This is just where we worship him on earth.'

Burt's heart sank. It sounded like God was the king of heaven. Where on earth was that? Not in here by the looks of things.

'I need to speak to God. It's very important. There's a monster on the loose in the woods nearby.'

The vicar found this funny. 'Don't be silly, there's no such thing as monsters and you'll only find heaven when you die. All you can do is be the best that you can be and pray everyday so that God will look after you. Now come on in – you're blocking the door.'

'There is such a thing as monsters, and I need to know if God will help me fight them.'

'Look, the service is about to start. Would you like to come in or not?'

Burt entered with Sandy trotting by his side.

Er, no I'm sorry, I'm afraid I can't let you in with your dog. You'll have to tie her up outside.'

'This is Sandy my guide dog and we are best friends.'

'Well, it would be different if you really were blind, but I'm afraid I can't make any exceptions … Oh hello, Mrs Weatherall.'

The old lady he'd met before shuffled past him tutting. 'You'll have to watch this one,' she said. 'He's full of questions and he needs a good smack.'

'Actually, I do have one question, Sir,' Burt asked the vicar. 'Can you tell me who God is and what he does and how I can talk to him?'

'God is love. God is good. God is your guide. He lives inside all of us. He is the light, my child.'

Burt decided he needed to think a bit more about this, but he had one more question: 'Why are some things horrible for no reason?'

'Ah, you want to know about evil. The truth is we're all a mix of good and bad and we have to choose what we will do.'

'And what are good and evil?'

'Good is trying to help other people and evil is trying to hurt them. A good person tries to make others feel happy, which makes them feel happy in turn. And they feel bad if they hurt somebody's feelings because they have something called a conscience. A conscience means you think about other people's feelings.

'Bad people think only of themselves; they don't care about other people at all. They hurt other people to get something they want, or just to make themselves feel bigger and better. And they do it so much they start to enjoy it. That's evil.'

Burt had come across this in bullies at school.

'Thank you. I think I understand.'

'Good, now my flock is waiting. Are you coming in or not, young man?'

'Er, I think I can hear my parents calling. I have to go now. Goodbye.'

Burt made for a gate on the far side of the courtyard but when the vicar had disappeared, he turned and studied the church.

The spire pointed up into the sky and Burt looked up to see if he could see heaven in the clouds. For a second he thought he could see a big, bearded face like Santa's but it blew away to reveal the bright hot sun, which dazzled him so much he could see it when he closed his eyes.

God must live in the sun where rainbows come from, Burt thought, *but no one knows because you can't look at it.* He thought about telling the people in the church to come out and look at the sky, but they were all singing and talking as one.

He sat down on a grassy verge and thought about it some more. In the end he decided God must be made out of everyone you love and their love for you gets all rolled up inside you. The people who love you want what's best for you and you can use their goodwill as an example to guide you. And if God is our guide and that voice is

33

inside, maybe there is a part of yourself you can follow, above all else.

So Burt listened to himself and made up his own mind. He wanted to find his very own tree and build a tree house. But he had to find this monster first and put it in its place, so his friends would be safe when they came to play. For, although he looked like a little boy, Burt Marshmallow was a warrior now.

6

The Hollow Tree

Burt and Sandy turned tail and left the churchyard and the first thing they noticed was a stream flowing out of the hill. Burt knew that meant that there must be a river at the end – Ghastly had said that the monster lived by an enchanted river in the woods.

They played games as they walked down the hill and at the bottom Burt spied with his little eye something beginning with T. It was the oldest-looking tree he had ever seen, and it was leaning over the stream.

It was twisted and gnarled but it had two branches that looked like two arms stretching out of its sides. But they were too steep to hold a tree house. Even more remarkably it had a big gaping hole like a mouth in its trunk, so that the tree looked exactly like it was waking up and yawning.

Burt remembered his dad saying that the family tree gave him advice, so he thought he'd try his luck with this one. It looked friendly enough.

'Hello,' he said to the tree, 'could you tell me where all of your friends live?'

The tree didn't say a word, which is what normally happens when you try to talk to trees.

Then Burt saw a bright-red squirrel in the branches over his head. It ran down the length of one branch, spiralling round and round until it reached the tree trunk, where it came to rest. It sat there and from nowhere produced an acorn, which it held to its mouth and nibbled.

Burt thought that it looked like it was eating a big Easter egg whole. It nibbled on the top with its big front teeth and munched. He watched it nibble away like that for a little while and he realised he was hungry. So he picked up an acorn he saw on the ground, and tried it for himself.

'Yuck!' he exclaimed as he spat it out. 'Why are you eating that?' he asked the squirrel. 'It's horrible.'

Well, that did it, because the squirrel got a fright, or maybe it was insulted, because it sprinted off into the great tree's mouth. Burt went closer to say sorry and to see where it had gone; then, without warning, the great tree spat the squirrel out and it ran away.

Burt peeked inside and to his surprise he found a picnic basket lodged in the trunk. Finders keepers, Burt thought, and helped himself. This was clearly a present from the tree.

When he looked in the basket Burt was treated to a mouth-watering sight. There was such a lot of food inside, it could have fed an army. He ate chicken legs and ham sandwiches and sausage rolls and crisps and then a big slice of chocolate cake for pudding, which was Burt's favourite food in the whole wide world. And of course he shared it with Sandy, who ate even more than him.

He drank delicious apple juice and when he'd had his fill he stuffed his pockets with biscuits. He kept a flask full of drink for later and a picnic blanket to keep him warm. But he couldn't carry it all and he didn't want to be greedy so he gave the rest back to the tree.

He decided this tree was very friendly, so he tried his luck again. It had clearly woken up. He stood up and faced it and cleared his throat.

'Ahem. Thank you very much for all that lovely food. I have to go now because I'm trying to find the monster in the woods. Can you tell me which way to go next, please, sleepy tree? Should I just keep following the stream?'

There was total silence.

He stood there for ages but the tree said nothing and he felt exactly like he did when he was being ignored by a grown-up. So he turned and he was about to leave when he realised he was feeling quite drowsy. He decided to have a mid-morning nap for no particular reason.

'It must be all the food I've eaten. Sometimes being full makes me tired.'

He sat back against the tree and made himself cosy, all wrapped up and snug in the picnic blanket, then he closed his eyes and dreamed.

In his dreams Burt was in a boat floating the wrong way up a river. There were other people he knew, like Pigtails and his friends, passing him and asking him why he was floating the wrong way. 'It must be the currents sweeping him upstream,' his daddy was saying, then he saw his mummy crying and Burt wanted to comfort her, but he couldn't think of anything to say.

So instead he took out a paddle and he struggled up the river. Pretty soon he was all alone. The river got narrower and shallower and turned into a brook. Then finally he disappeared from view altogether, into a tunnel under the ground.

Burt paddled furiously in the dark and he became very frightened, but there was a light at the end of the tunnel. And when he came out he noticed he was now following a stream. He came to rest right there under the yawning old tree.

'Hello,' the tree said, putting its hands on its hips. 'I've been expecting you, Burt.'

'How do you know my name?'

'Because I've met you of course. Look down and you'll see what I mean.'

Well, under the tree do you know what Burt saw? It was a little boy sleeping who looked exactly like him, with Sandy standing guard and staring straight at him.

'Hello, Burt,' she said. 'This tree is going to help.'

Then he looked down and he saw he was a man! He had grown up in his dreams and travelled back to where it all began. The church on the hill was where he was christened as a baby. And he knew this tree would help him.

'Can you tell me which way to go, sleepy tree?' he asked again. 'I'm afraid I've got lost; I've forgotten where I am. I'm stuck here all alone and I don't know what to do.'

'Well then, it's a good job I'm here,' the sleepy tree said cheerfully. And on hearing its voice Burt could tell it was going to tell the truth.

'In a little while your stream will disappear underground, where you can't follow it. The wild wood lies on a different path. We trees call it Wood-Land. So open your eyes and find your own way, but first let me say this: you will find that your mind works in mysterious ways; you just have to learn to follow the signs. And if you ever get lost, just ask for directions; there's always someone willing to help.'

With that Burt found himself wrapped up in a blanket. He stood up and a strange wind blew down the valley and caught the blanket like a sail. It blew Burt forward and when he turned around he saw the branches of the tree were pointing like a signpost. The tree was telling him which way to go.

Well, one branch pointed back to the church where Burt had come from, and Burt knew that backwards was always the wrong way. The other one reached out above his head and pointed along the hillside. And that's when Burt saw it: there was another tree on the horizon.

He could just make out the outline; the rest was all in shadow. But he could see it was shaped like a V, because it had two tree trunks growing at angles from one hole in the ground. As he looked at it some more he could see the branches were all entangled, which made it look like a heart.

He knew, of course, that was his next port of call, even though it meant leaving his stream.

It was then that Burt woke up with a start.

7

Learning to Climb

The tree really did look like a signpost and there really was a tree on the horizon just like in his dream. Was nature on his side or was it all in his mind? Burt felt the natural world was calling to him.

He gave the sleepy tree a big hug and promised to return. Then he wrapped his blanket around his shoulders a bit like a cape and threaded the belt on his trousers through the handle of his flask. Finally he found a big stick like the one the old lady had used for walking. This, he thought, would make the going easier, especially because he was straying so far off the beaten track.

At last they arrived and stopped for a rest, and he and Sandy discussed what they should do next. Burt knew he needed directions so he asked but got no answers. Then he heard a funny chirping noise. The tree was full of pretty singing birds.

Well, birds like trees and they fly up in the sky. They would have seen Wood-Land with their bird's-eye view. There was only one thing for it; he knew he had to learn some time. Burt would have to learn to climb, so he could go and speak with the birds.

He left his things for Sandy to guard and climbed up to the nearest branch. He grabbed a hold and lifted himself up, then looked carefully around for a higher branch. In this way he climbed up the tree like a ladder, picking the highest branch within his reach each time until about halfway up he made a discovery.

He had pulled himself on to a big thick branch and up above him was a lumpy thing swarming with bees. It was a beehive where the bees make their honey.

Well, this was quite dangerous. Burt was hanging on to a branch a long way above the ground and the bees thought he'd come to steal their honey. So they buzzed around his head and he got stung several times.

Burt was determined. He shouted for Sandy to watch out and swiped his hand and knocked the beehive out of the tree. The bees buzzed furiously and he got stung again, but they moved away eventually. The pain made his eyes water and Burt stayed where he was for a bit. He wasn't going to let a little thing like that stop him, though, so he gathered up his courage and kept climbing.

Higher and higher Burt climbed until he came to the top. This was where the singing birds had been perched, but as he approached they flew off.

Burt had no choice now. He tried to see the woods for himself but there were branches and twigs and leaves everywhere, so he struggled to his feet to get a better view. He clutched at a thin branch and clung on to it swaying in the wind, and he stretched as high up as he could.

Then he saw something. Not the woods but a bird's nest, which is a bit like a tree house for birds. A mother bird sat in it and she didn't fly off.

Then she started singing a beautiful melody. Burt listened entranced and he was so happy, he almost forgot there was work to do.

'Excuse me, sorry for interrupting. I think your singing is beautiful. I was wondering if I could ask you a question ...'

The mother bird cocked her head and waited.

'You must know all about the lie of the land from when you're flying. Would you mind telling me where the woods are, please? So I can find the tallest tree and build my own nest in the sky.'

Well, the bird started singing a different tune now and it was even more beautiful than before. It sounded happy and lovely and exciting, but Burt didn't know what it meant. So at last the bird took off and flew and he peered after her and called for her to come back. Then it struck him: she was showing him the way he had to go.

Burt couldn't very well fly after her so he looked for a landmark to head towards. And the first thing he saw was a big stone bridge in the valley ahead.

'And where there's a bridge, there's a river!' he said out loud.

He was about to set off when he noticed three pretty eggs in the nest that the mother bird had left. He thought he had better wait until she returned to keep them safe. And it's a good job he did because after a while there was a scuffling noise, and Burt heard a creature climbing up the tree.

Burt was flabbergasted when he realised what it was. It was a fairy carrying a sack full of eggs. It must be Flutterby, the fairy the ghost had told him about.

'Ooh, another nest. Good haul today.'

'Oh no you don't!' Burt said.

'Oh, ow, what, hey? What's this, a monkey?! In England – I say!'

Flutterby hadn't seen Burt and the fairy got such a fright it nearly dropped its swag.

'You had better put those bird eggs back. Those are babies you've stuffed in that sack.'

Burt decided immediately that he wasn't going to let Flutterby get away, but he couldn't reach it from here, certainly not without risking damage to the eggs. Then he had a bright idea. He started whistling, as Pigtails had once taught him, only this time he made it sound like birdsong.

In actual fact, it really was birdsong. Burt discovered he could speak the language of the birds. And he told them all about the nasty fairy and what it was doing to their eggs.

It wasn't long before a whole flock of birds swooped down on them. They pecked at Flutterby and plucked the sack away and some came and perched on Burt's head and shoulders to watch. Then they picked the fairy up and whisked it away, and the only bird left sat by his ear. It was the mother bird that had showed him the way.

She sang to him again, softly this time. She sang a beautiful song just for him. And Burt understood every word.

'Hello, my name's Starling,' she said. 'The birds are your friends forever after what you've done; you just saved our children. That fairy has been poaching our eggs all season. Please let us repay you. We can guide you to your tree. I'll never forget what you've done for us and what you did for me!'

'I know there is a monster waiting for you and I don't know how to help you in your fight, but I can help you build your tree house because we birds are good at building nests.'

Burt sat there a while and talked with Starling about the tree house of his dreams, and she taught him the secrets of building nests. 'First,' she said, 'you find a good solid branch like this. Then you take lots of twigs and weave them together like a basket. Next you pad it with leaves which you pluck from the trees, and finally you line it with colourful feathers that other birds give as nest-warming presents.

They sat there for what felt like forever until eventually Burt had to go. Starling said she'd be watching over him on his journey and Burt told her he was sad he had to go, but he knew he had a mission to fulfil and he was worried about Sandy.

'These monsters won't biff themselves, Starling!' he said as he departed.

45

So he climbed down and at the bottom of the tree found Sandy eating honey from the hive. It seemed the bees had long since departed, so Burt tucked in as well.

8

Burt's Big Fight

The going was easier for a while after that and Burt and Sandy made good progress for the rest of the day. Burt followed the contours of the land to the big stone bridge and the birds flying overhead kept him heading the right way.

They stopped once or twice for a rest and Burt snacked on crushed biscuits and honey. It was on one of these occasions that Starling came and spoke to him again. He offered her some food but she said there was no time: she had come to warn them of danger ahead.

The birds had spotted a troll in the undergrowth near the road bridge. She warned him not to travel on the road because it lay in wait, ready to ambush little boys and girls.

'Hmm,' said Burt, 'I'd better find some rocks to bring. I'll sneak up close with my catapult and put a stop to this.'

He walked until he saw the road, which was lined with a dry-stone wall. Then he crawled along behind the wall so that no one could see him from the other side. As he went he picked up lots of little stones and put them in the empty flask on his belt.

The road was quiet, just a few family cars driving this way and that. When he was close to the bridge Burt peaked over carefully but he couldn't see the troll. Then the birds sang to him to move further down. The troll was on the other side of the road behind a bush with pink flowers on it.

This was difficult. He peeked and saw the bush rustling and twitching but he couldn't get a clear shot at the troll. So he tried throwing a stone on the road to make it think something was there and come out. But it didn't work – the troll was waiting for the smell of children travelling on their own.

Burt decided to do something brave and rather dangerous. Leaving Sandy there to wait for him, he crept back away from the bridge. When he was a safe distance away he climbed over the wall. He was going to use himself as bait.

He walked along the road casually with his arms behind his back, whistling as if he didn't have a care in the world. And as he got close to the bridge, sure enough, the troll leapt out to scare him.

'Oi, you there! Where do ya think you're going? Little boys alone have got to pay my bridge toll if they wanna live to tell the tale. I calls this children's tax, you see, and you'd better cough up quick. My name's Trevor the troll, and I don't like little boys at all.'

Burt just stood there looking at the troll with his

hands behind his back. And what do you think he had behind there?

'Come on, come here or you'll get a smack. You'd better give me everything you've got, you little snot. What's that behind your back?'

'My name is Burt Marshmallow,' Burt said at last, 'and I've got surprise for you.'

'Ooh I like surprises!'

Burt whipped out the catapult with a stone at the ready and before the stupid troll could even blink he had shot him between the eyes. Trevor the troll staggered back and forth for a moment and then plonked down on his backside. *Ouch!*

Burt loaded another bigger stone and advanced. The first one had just been a pebble to stun him.

'You're going to take me to your stash. I want to see all of the things you've stolen.'

'Oh mercy me! What have I done to deserve this, eh?'

'It's because you're horrible and no one wants to play with you.'

He marched the troll to a gate, where Sandy joined them. The gate led to a slope beside the bridge that was covered in thick undergrowth. Burt had to be extra careful that he didn't lose his prisoner. After a short while they reached a fallen tree that was snapped and hollowed out. It looked like a banana with the insides scooped out and it was full of all manner of children's things.

There were sweeties and toys and school bags with lunchboxes and pencil cases and storybooks to read, all stacked high in two big bin bags. Burt

kept the troll in his sights the whole time and made sure its big strong arms were out of reach so he couldn't make a grab for him.

'What do you need all this stuff for? I bet you don't even like sweets and toys and school stuff because you're too horrible to have any fun. And I bet you can't read, even though you're a grown-up.'

Well, that touched a nerve. 'Shut your face, you horrible little SWOT!' The troll lunged forward, leaving Burt no time to aim. He fired the rock off at close range instinctively and it hit the troll square between the legs.

'Oooooooooooooooooooooohhhhhhhhhhhhhhhhhhhh!' … was all it could say as its knees knocked together and it fell face down on the floor.

Burt loaded another rock and waited for it to recover. He knew now that this troll didn't like children because they had fun and were cleverer than he was. When at last Trevor stumbled to his feet Burt had decided what to do with him. He made the troll pick up both the bin bags and marched him back to the road, bringing Sandy along as well.

Out of the hoard of treasure he pulled first one skipping rope, then another – presumably stolen from little girls – and used these to tie the troll to a lamppost.

Next Burt made a pile of all the things the troll had stolen beside the lamppost for people to collect.

Finally he fished around in the school bags for paper and a felt-tip pen to use for making a sign.

It read:

> This is Trevor the river troll.
> He hides under bridges and steals from children.
> Please take what's yours and tell him what you think of him.
> Yours faithfully,
> Burt Marshmallow

Then he pinned it to the troll's chest with a safety pin he found, and he left him there wailing.

'But please, you don't understand, if the adults see me I'll turn into stone. That's why I have to get children on their own.'

Burt didn't really care if that was true. He was busy thinking about what lay ahead. From now on he'd keep his flask full of rocks and his catapult at the ready. Things were getting dangerous.

He rooted through the pile of stolen treasure and took some things he needed. He took a big black rucksack which had no name on it and he filled it with the food and drink from all of the lunch boxes. Finally he took a blue plastic raincoat as well, just in case. He was sure whoever owned it would understand.

It was getting late so Burt thanked the birds for their warning and they all came and perched on the troll to keep guard. Burt thought this was funny because it meant Trevor got all covered in bird poo like a statue in the park. And that's exactly what he turned into as soon as the first car passed. Trevor hadn't been lying, because when a grown up-looked out the window, Trevor yelled one last time and turned to stone.

It was a remarkable sight – a stone troll tied to a lamppost with a stone tablet sign and a miserable face. Ever since it has served as a reminder to river trolls everywhere and confused many an adult as they drove their cars by. And of course, from then on, Burt was famous because he'd signed his name on the statue.

9

The River of Dreams

Burt didn't know what to do now. It was getting quite late and he was very hungry, so he decided he would find somewhere to camp. He hoped his parents weren't worried about him – though of course they were.

The only place he could think to go was the undergrowth by the bridge, so he found his way back to the fallen tree.

He and Sandy shared jam sandwiches and cheese and ham sandwiches and pickled onions and crisps, which was a bit of a strange evening meal, especially for Sandy.

Then Burt climbed into the tree as if it was a bed and wrapped up warm in his blanket. He used his bag as a pillow and fell straight asleep, He was so tired from all the exercise and excitement.

The tree log was about the length of a bed and it was resting on a slope, as I've said. But the way it had fallen, it had landed on a rock, and it rested on the rock like a seesaw. There it had stayed until it rotted hollow so that now it looked more like a baby's cot, rocking to and fro.

Burt slept happily inside and everything was fine. But Sandy was restless. She hopped in at Burt's feet to huddle up and join his peaceful slumber, but then with a slip and a rickety-rock the scales were turned. As you can imagine a big dog jumping in caused the log to tip, and with Sandy sitting in the front end as if she was setting off on a drive, it slipped off the rock and started off down the slope. It slid faster and faster until it went so fast Sandy's cheeks got blown out from her face. And it weaved this way and that, slaloming between the trees. And all the while Burt remained fast asleep and dreamed he was sledging down a snowy hill.

Then at the bottom the slope levelled out on to a bay of little stones and they scattered and rolled as the log slid over them. This slowed the log down and it was launched gently like a boat into the river.

From the bridge they would have looked like a giant Poohstick floating underneath.

Sandy panted and watched aghast as they danced their way down the river and were swept away. Soon the river calmed and the log boat drifted gently, rocking to and fro. And Burt dreamed every dream he had ever had that night, as he floated along unaware of the world. They all merged together into one magical dream of adventure and mystery and monsters and victory, in which Burt was the saviour of the whole wide world.

Eventually Sandy fell asleep, snuggling up to Burt, and if they had kept on like that all night, they would have been swept into the sea. But the log washed up on an island, which split the river in two.

In the morning Burt woke up and stretched. Oh, he felt very stiff and bruised. What an uncomfortable bed that had been! Then he looked around for Sandy, but she was nowhere to be seen.

Where is she? he thought. Then he rubbed the sleep out of his eyes and looked again. Come to think of it, where am I!?

He was sitting in an old hollow tree, which he remembered. But now it was tangled up in a pile of slimy logs in the middle of a river! He got up and grabbed his things and scrambled up the log pile to look around. And there ahead was Sandy on a sandy island with a strange-looking creature. She had made a friend.

'This is Mr Otter,' Sandy informed him when he'd worked his way to the bay.

'Oh right, hello. How are you?' Burt asked Sandy.

'Oh, very well, thank you. I'm right as rain.'

Then Burt did a double-take. Sandy had just spoken to him! And what on earth was this strange, furry, whiskery creature?

An otter, Sandy called it.

It had webbed feet like a duck, but it looked more like a cat with a funny fat tail. And Sandy was talking to it and it was talking back.

Burt felt faint so he sat down to gather himself. What on earth was going on? Then he saw a big pile of stinking fish guts and fish heads. Sandy and

Mr Otter were eating them for breakfast. Now he felt sick as well.

'Don't worry, young man; we've saved some for you,' Mr Otter said as it dropped a fish in front of him.

Burt looked at it for a moment. It was twitching and staring at him.

'Sorry,' Burt said at last, partly to the dying fish and partly to Mr Otter. 'I'm not hungry, thank you.' This was a lie but you're allowed to lie a bit if you're being polite.

'Suit yourself,' Mr Otter replied. And it took it in its paws and bit it in half, giving the tail end to Sandy. 'More for us, eh, old bean?'

Uugghh. 'Excuse me, how did you get all of these fish? And why don't you cook them first?'

'In answer to your first question, I swim down deep and I grab them with my teeth.' Mr Otter opened his mouth to show a row of pointy teeth with fishy bits sticking out.

'Oooh.'

'And in answer to your second question: cooking fish is a travesty committed only by human beings, except for the Japanese, that is. Have you never heard of sushi? Raw fish and rice, I believe; a fine cuisine.'

Burt had not heard of sushi and he didn't want to by the sound of it, but he had just got very excited, too excited to argue or pay attention.

'Wait a minute. Did you say you can swim deep down in the water faster than a fish? Could you teach me?'

'Hmmm. Well, I'm all for good manners where guests are concerned but if you don't mind me saying, you're rather ill-suited to swimming. You don't have a tail or webbed feet for propulsion, or oiled fur for warmth, and how are you supposed to catch a fish with that little mouth of yours? Your teeth look quite blunt.

'No, it's not like playing tag, you know. This is a serious business and one must be specially adapted and trained for the job like my youngsters. It's quite an impossible task, I'm afraid.'

As if on cue two young otters waddled over.

'I'm taking my boy and girl here for a lesson now as it happens. Swish, Netty, this is Sandy the ... dog, I believe, and ...'

The old otter stared at Burt for a moment.

'Oh, I'm Burt Marshmallow ... the human being. Pleased to meet you.

The young otters said hello and seemed quite shy.

'What an odd name you have,' Mr Otter said. 'You humans! But as they say, humans are animals, too. Oh, I do beg your pardon, I'm Humperdink. Pleasure to make your acquaintance. Well, we must be off. Lunch won't catch itself, as I always say.

'Come along, Netty. Don't dawdle, Swish.'

'Wait, err, ... I brought you a gift. All the way from ... Japan.'

'No! Really? Oh, how thoughtful. How dreadfully kind. What is it?'

'Erm. It's over here. It's a Japanese ... warship.'

He took them over and showed them the hollow log he'd floated up in.

'Wow!' the kids shouted as they jumped on board.

'Oh, my Lord. Good gracious. Does that float on top of the water? And you can ride inside it? A warship you say. Hmmm. I don't know about war but we could carry the fish to the woods to trade, and we could take the kids on holidays. ... Oh, what a remarkable present, I can't wait to tell the wife. You must meet her. Stay for dinner, we're having...'

'Raw fish. Yeah, I don't like that.'

'Oh, but I must return the favour. This is too much. Erm, would you like me to teach you how to swim?'

'Oh, yes please!' Burt said delighted.

This, of course, had been his plan all along. He knew from giving presents to his mum that she was always nice to him afterwards.

So for the next few hours Humperdink tried to teach him to swim, first telling him to put his fingers and toes together so that they worked better as paddles. The only problem was that, try as he might, he couldn't master the otters' swimming stroke. His body was simply the wrong shape.

You see, the otters used their little arms to paddle and wag their big thick tails to change direction. Then they kicked their little webbed feet and shot off like a motor-powered submarine. But Burt didn't have little arms, a big strong tail or even webbed feet. He kept on sinking to the riverbed and needed Humperdink to save him, which got quite embarrassing.

So he decided to try a new approach by learning to swim from Sandy instead. Sandy tried to teach him the doggie paddle and he could do it but he found it very tiring. And it meant he could only swim on the surface and not very far at all.

Then, after several days of trying like this, Burt awoke on his sandy bed to see a frog hopping about in front of him.

It looked at him and said, 'Hello, lovely, give us a kiss good morning.' Then it hopped over and Burt uncertainly gave it a peck on its slimy green cheek.

'Why did you want a kiss?' he asked. 'Are you going to turn into a princess?'

'No way, I just wanted a kiss,' it said, then it hopped off into the water.

Sandy awoke and ran after the frog because she liked chasing things like that but the frog swam so fast it escaped easily.

This gave Burt an idea. He tried swimming like the frog, and do you know what? That stroke worked best for him. He called it the 'froggy paddle'. 'What you do,' Burt explained to Sandy, 'is hop into the water shouting *ribbit, ribbit* as you go. Then you reach your arms out and around a bit like you're drawing out wings. And you kick your legs out to the side and back in, just like the frog did.'

The kick made him move real quick!

He found he could swim on the surface like this,

with his head bobbing up and down to breathe. But with a bit more practice he could also dive down and watch the otters chasing the fish. He was soon an even faster swimmer than Sandy and he could swim just as far as she could, although the otters were still the best swimmers of all. Burt wished he had a big tail like them.

So that's how Burt learned to swim.

They were ready to leave the island now, but before they swam off into the sunset, he thought he'd better ask Humperdink where Wood-Land was.

'Have you heard of it? I'm on a quest to root out the evil there and to find the tallest tree.'

Wood-Land? Oh my dear boy, that's just downstream. Oh yes, my friends there have told me all about the evil that dwells in those woods. It hunts the animals you know. Frightful. I sell my fish in Wood-Land when I get a good catch, you see. Just follow the river and you can't miss it. But I must ask, are you quite sure you know what you're doing?'

'Of course! I must be going now. Thank you for all you've taught me.'

'It was my pleasure. But don't say I didn't warn you. Fare thee well, noble squire. Good luck on your quest! … Adieu. I do hope I see you again. Say goodbye, Netty, Swish.'

'Goodbye, Burt, goodbye Sandy.'

'Goodbye!' Burt and Sandy cried, as they sploshed off the island and swam away.

10

The Fisherman's Hut

Burt had wrapped his rucksack and stick and some of his clothes in his raincoat so that they kept dry, and he used it like a float so that the river did most of the work. It wasn't long before they entered Wood-Land territory. The trees grew big and wild, tall and thick, and they hung over the river on both sides, almost closing off the sky. But it was getting ever colder and in the gap above Burt could see rainclouds gathering.

He looked about for a suitable place to swim ashore. Then he heard a deep voice singing a pretty song somewhere up ahead:

> Thou shall have a fishy
> On a little dishy
> Thou shall have a fishy
> When the boat comes in.
>
> Dance for your daddy
> Sing for your mammy
> Dance for your daddy
> To your mammy sing.

Thou shall have a fishy
On a little dishy
Thou shall have a fishy
When the boat comes in.

As he floated in the water entranced by the melody, something colourful landed on his makeshift float. At first he thought it was a dragon fly or something, then he saw it was attached to some fine string, which quickly became entangled around his things.

He looked up and saw the source of the line and of course the song. It was a man sitting on the riverbank amid the trees with a big fishing rod and a fisherman's net.

'Damn and Blast, snagged again. Just my luck, what is it this time? More driftwood? Hang on a minute, what's this? Well, well, this river does throw up some surprises. ... Now then, young'un. Just wait there, let me reel you in. You're tangled in my line. Oh an' a dog too, my my. Ha-ha. Hellooo, little fishies ... You look like you need some warm clothes and a good feed: fancy swimming in a river way out here on your own.'

A good feed certainly sounded appealing. Burt was famished because he'd finished off the last of his food the day before.

'Thank you! I'm Burt and this is Sandy,' Burt called across to the riverbank.

Just as he reached the shore and started untangling the fisherman's line the storm cloud broke and it started pouring with rain.

63

'Well, that's done it. No more fishing today. You'll catch your death if we don't get you inside. Let's get some supper in ya, laddie.'

Burt was in no mood to argue. He hadn't been indoors for a long time and he missed the family fire and feeling warm and cosy.

'Do you have a cooker to cook the food?' He was looking at a bucket of raw fish the fisherman carried.

'Oh yes, I have a stove for cooking and it'll dry you off and warm you right through. Do you know how to make a fire?'

'I don't,' Burt confessed.

'We'll soon mend that.'

The fisherman fed Sandy some of his fish and led them deep into the woods towards his hut.

The fisherman's hut was made of brown logs and had a roof painted green like leaves, making it difficult to see in the undergrowth. As he got closer he saw it had a chimney pot, a door and a window, but it was only about as big as his room at home.

'Here, Sandy, you help yourself,' the fisherman said, putting more fish into a big dog bowl.

Then he opened the door and guided Burt inside. A thought occurred to Burt as they went in.

'Is this like a tree house on the ground?'

'Yes, you could say that. Now let's get a fire going and get you changed.'

The stove stood directly in front of them in the middle of the room. It was a metal cylinder with a big door in the side where you put the wood and cooked the food, and a metal tube that took the

smoke up to the chimney. The fisherman dropped his things on the bed at the back of the room and handed Burt his clothes.

The fisherman beckoned him over and showed him how to make a fire. He had seen a fire made many times but he wasn't allowed to touch matches. This was the first fire Burt ever lit.

While Burt was transfixed by the jumping flames and pleasant warmth, the fisherman stood up and moved to the door. The lock clicked and immediately Sandy started barking outside. It was then that Burt looked up and saw something he hadn't noticed before.

There was a large grey dog under the fisherman's bed. It was staring at him and it started growling. Now he knew he had been tricked.

'That's my dog, Wolf,' the fisherman said. 'You don't want to get on the wrong side of him.'

Didn't Ghastly the Ghost have a dog called Wolf? Was this him?

Sandy started scratching at the door and whining outside as Burt turned slowly around. He was afraid to look because he knew what he would see. The fisherman was a man all right but he could see the monster in his eyes. He gave him that hungry, excited look and it seemed to carry a terrible threat.

'You'd best cook me my dinner, boy, or I'll give you a smack. And you'd better get used to doing my chores because you're staying here with me from now on. I'm your new daddy, you see.'

66

'No, you are not. I've got a daddy already.'

'Well, he didn't look after you very well, did he? Letting you get lost like this.'

'My daddy's good. I came here on my own to build a tree house like his and to fight monsters, and now I know that means you! If me and Sandy don't get you, my daddy will.'

'Let me explain something to you. You will never find your way home from here. And they'll never find you here either. I'm afraid you'll never see the light of day again. From now on you're stuck with me. So you'd better get used to it.'

'I don't need anyone's help. I'll get you myself. And Sandy will get me home.'

'Ah yes, well, I'll have to take care of her, won't I?'

'If you so much as touch her you'll regret it, I promise.'

'What are you going to do? I'm much bigger and older than you. There's only one thing you need to know and that's do exactly as I say … or else!'

'Well, of course, Burt didn't like that. He ran forward and hit the fisherman but the fisherman hit him back!

'I see your daddy didn't teach you any manners. We'll see if we can't do something about that and shut that big mouth of yours. Or are you going to do as you're told and make me something to eat?'

Burt's catapult and stick were on the bed guarded by Wolf, so Burt didn't have any choice. He knew how to cook and clean a bit from helping his mum around the house. So he started chopping fish and vegetables and he cooked them both some dinner. He needed time to think and regain his strength.

When he was finished the fisherman grunted contentedly. Then he got up to leave.

'Wolf will keep an eye on you while I deal with that dog of yours. She's making a racket and no mistake.'

The fisherman fetched his net from the bed and Wolf advanced on Burt, who backed away into the corner. The fisherman left, locking the door behind him.

Burt heard a scuffle but Sandy it seemed got the better of him, for soon he heard her scampering away as she tried to escape the fisherman's horrid, grasping hands. Then he heard her bark:

'Burt, you must get away now. I'll hold him off for as long as I can.'

'Sandy!' Burt shouted.

He looked around the room and his gaze settled on the monstrous creature in front of him. The stove fire glowed behind Wolf so that its pointy ears lit up like big, red horns. It was baring its teeth in an awful snarl and its hellish eyes held only hatred.

'You are mine now, little boy. I'm going to gobble you up,' it said in its most menacing voice.

'Well, I think your master would be very upset. I'm to look after you both and clean up your mess.'

'Some master! He gave my dinner to that dog of yours to keep her quiet. She thinks you're something special. Well, let's see how special you taste.'

The dog advanced towards him until it was within striking distance and Burt should have been scared but all he could think of was poor Sandy. Then he remembered her treats. They were in his pocket.

'I taste like raw fish, the same as all little boys. But I suppose you know that, living with a monster.'

The dog stopped and seemed to choke. 'I don't! He's never let me eat child before. All I get is fish guts and heads! Yak!'

'So you've only ever eaten fish? That must be horrible. I was starving before but I still hated eating raw fish.'

'Tell me about it.'

'Oh you know what? I have some of Sandy's special food in my pocket. It gives her magical powers. Here.'

'Oh ... wow. That's like ... like ... the food I dream about. It tastes like ...'

'They're made out of sunlight. That's where the special flavour and magical powers come from.'

'Wow. Can I have another one?'

'Of course.'

Well, good cos I could just take them all if I wanted to.'

'Well, of course you could but then you'd never know what they tasted like cooked like human food.'

'Cooked!? I've never had anything cooked before.'

'Really? Well, that's what unlocks the magic and makes you better at fighting. That's why humans are in charge and get to order you around. Because they eat cooked food.'

'I knew it must be something like that. I'm sick of doing what I'm told all the time.'

'Yeah, tell me about it. Would you like me to cook you one?'

'No, I'd like you to cook me all of them. Go on. Get to the stove and put them all in.'

Burt went over to the open stove and put the treats on the cooking shelf.

'Oh wow, just smell that!'

'Um, bloomin' marvellous.'

The dog was slavering and drooling and it barged Burt out of the way to smell the treats.

The smell drifted out of the stove and the dog couldn't resist. It stuck its head right inside to get at the treats. Burt, anticipating the horrid dog's greed, had already stepped behind it, and as it put its front legs in the oven to reach the ones at the back, ignoring the heat, Burt grabbed its hind legs and pushed it right in. Then he slammed the door shut.

He felt a little bad about this, I must admit. But it was going to eat him so he had no choice.

He needn't have bothered feeling sorry for it, though. The monster's dog was evil and Burt was very good. In fact, this dog was made out of pure evil. And coincidentally Burt Marshmallow was made out of pure good, which was the source of his increasingly magical powers.

You see, Burt had lit this fire and anyone who knows anything about magic will tell you a fire you build burns with the passion of your soul. So this was in fact a very dangerous experiment. Burt had put pure evil into the fires of his soul.

The stove started shaking so Burt knew something was wrong. He ran to the table where the fisherman had eaten, threw it over, and took cover just in time.

Then ... BOOOOOOOOOOOOOOOOOOOOOOOOOM! It had exploded.

The stove shot fire from its bottom and fired off like a rocket through the chimney, leaving a big gaping hole in the roof. Burt was covered in soot and his eyebrows were burnt off.

He opened his eyes and was flabbergasted to see the rocket shooting higher and higher through the hole in the roof. Then without warning it exploded like a firework. The biggest firework you have ever seen. It glowed with all the colours of the rainbow and stained the sky red.

Every creature in Wood-Land must have seen that, Burt thought to himself, including the monstrous fisherman. There was no time to lose. He had to get out of here. He grabbed his things, then he looked around to see what else he could use. He found a flashlight and a length of rope. Then he grabbed all the food and water he could carry and packed everything in his rucksack.

The hole in the roof was quite high up but thankfully Burt was very good at climbing now. He picked up the table he'd hidden behind and put it where the stove had been. He climbed on top, then he reached up to the edge, grabbed on and swung himself up.

He stood on the roof and looked around with his flashlight but he couldn't see Sandy anywhere, so he slid off the roof and hopped down to the ground.

11

Wood-Land

By now Burt Marshmallow was no stranger to danger, but even he found Wood-Land scary at night. There were shadows and strange noises everywhere and Burt was always jumping and waving his flashlight around to see what was there.

He kept tripping up as he walked so he found it easier to crawl like an animal. Then he decided to be brave and turn off his torch so that the monster wouldn't see him coming. Pretty soon his eyes adapted to the light and he looked around for a clearing where he could camp beneath the stars. He had a feeling they would guide him.

At last he came to what looked like a break in the trees. Then he heard movement and turned on his torch and a set of eyes lit up. He was so jumpy he dropped the flashlight and he grabbed his catapult and fired, causing something to cry out in the night.

'OW! What the devil was that? Oh, goodness, gracious me, that hurt.'

Other voices followed:

'Help! Help! The Hunter has come.'

'Show yourself, you monster.'

Scarper everyone, I'll handle this.'

'Sorry!' Burt called out, realising his mistake. He had fired without checking if it was friend or foe. He'd been so jumpy, he'd jumped to the wrong conclusion – that whatever it was would be out to get him.

'What is all this racket? Order, order,' said an older voice.

It sounded like a leader.

'What is it?'

'Where is it?'

Burt realised he was covered in black soot and was almost invisible, so he picked up the flashlight. He had stumbled upon some kind of gathering of animals.

'That isn't the Hunter. It's a boy out in the woods at night. Bring the culprit forward at once. This is most peculiar.'

'Oh, Bernard, my dear, what a nasty bump. Are you OK, my darling? Oh, let me kiss it better for you.'

Burt shone the flashlight in the direction of the voices to see what he was dealing with. There seemed to be voices all around him and he was very confused.

'I'm blind. I've gone blind and I think I have concussion. That light must be his weapon. It's some kind of ray gun!'

'Oh, don't be such a cry-baby, Bernard. You're always moaning at the slightest thing.'

'Slightest thing! I've been shot with a ray gun. It's having a delayed effect! I think it's dissolving my insides.'

'Will you stop blinding us with that awful beam of light?! We have very sensitive eyes, you know.' The older voice belonged to a badger.

'Oh no, the monster is moving in for the kill,' a deer shouted.

'Aaarrrrgggghhhhh!' The cry baby was a rabbit.

Burt came closer, wondering whether there was anything he could do to calm things down.

'I'm not a monster. It was an accident,' he said.

He put his catapult away so as not to scare them, but he held onto his walking stick just in case.

'Take one more step and it will be your last, I assure you.'

Burt shone his flashlight down instinctively to see what had spoken to him. A fox leapt from view into a bush.

'He has some kind of light sabre. Animals, prepare to disband. Run!'

'Wait, wait, you will do no such thing. Stop panicking at once ... That's a torch you nincompoop!' It was the wise old badger again.

Burt turned off the flashlight.

We don't know he's a monster and we outnumber him. There's no such thing as a ray gun or a light sabre, you stupid fools. Do your jobs and bring the culprit forward at once.'

The fox reappeared riding a young male deer. They took his flashlight and marched him at antler

76

point into the centre of the clearing, where the badger stood holding conference and looking stern. He was standing upright and held a great wooden staff with a crystal ball at its head.

'Thanks to you lot, the Hunter will know exactly where we all are by now.'

'It's OK. I have intelligence that it's many miles from here.' The fox spoke in a proud tone. I want it known for the record that I was not afraid of that light. But the humans use many weapons. We cannot be too careful.'

'Who is the Hunter?' Burt enquired.

'Well, you should know!' the fox said. 'I was guarding his cabin to keep an eye on Wolf while Dawn followed the man towards the mountains. Then there was an explosion and a space rocket of some kind shot into the air. I saw this human leave through the roof shortly afterwards.'

'He must be his new servant! And he probably has even worse weapons than that terrible fire stick!' the hysterical rabbit shouted.

'Was it you that made the sky light up with fire?' enquired a quiet little mouse, pulling at his trouser leg.

'Who is the Hunter?' Burt repeated

'Why does this human speak our language?' said the fox.

The rabbits seemed to be keeping one eye on the fox as it spoke. Burt knew foxes ate rabbits. Why weren't these animals chasing each other like predator and prey? And why were they all gathered together? They must have declared a truce to discuss a problem of some kind. This was getting too confusing.

'This is true and most unusual. I've never known a human boy who could speak to the animals before; although I do know such a girl. But it can't be ...' The old badger's voice trailed off into a mutter.

'With all due respect, how do we know humans can't speak our language? Would you speak to the Hunter while he baited your family hole, Badger? This creature shot one of our men!' This voice sounded angry and impatient.

'Your accusation is noted, Captain Firebrand, but you think *everyone* is a monster. Need I remind you that I am Emissary of Wood-Land and I supersede your military rank? There is no evidence that he's on the monster's side. We know the Hunter takes children captive.'

'This boy may have been held against his will,; the old badger reasoned. 'Young man, explain yourself immediately. Why did you fire that shot at poor Bernard?'

I'm sorry, I was startled. And I was afraid it was another bad wolf, or else a fairy or a troll or something.'

'Another wolf? What do you mean? A fairy or a troll: what do you know of such things?'

'He lies! He is a human being. The killers of animals; destroyers of the natural world! I say we eat him before he does the same to us!'

Some of the assembled animals seemed to agree and were positively licking their lips at this thought.

Burt was beginning to make out what he was dealing with. It looked like there were a few of every type of animal in Wood-Land here, and they seemed to have him surrounded. He was thinking furiously.

Burt guessed the fisherman had been hunting the animals of Wood-Land as well, because a monster like him would be nasty to everything. The animals here must have gathered to decide what to do about it.

'I've come to attend the meeting. I have killed the Hunter's dog in the exploding fire but the Hunter has kidnapped a friend of mine. I'm afraid I think the Hunter is really a monster in disguise.'

'I thought all people were monsters!' observed the rabbit.

'Not at all,' said Burt. 'Some are nasty but most are nice.'

'What did your friend look like?' A female fox came forward and stood beside Firebrand, addressing the congregation. This was Dawn.

'She is a golden dog called Sandy. She is my guide and my closest friend and she led the monster away to save me.'

'I can vouch for the boy's story. The Hunter chased a yellow dog into one of his animal traps. I overheard him say that he was taking her and the boy to his cave.'

'Oh no, poor Sandy! ...' cried Burt. 'I have to help my friend.'

'You have to help yourself first, young man. There is much to explain,' the old badger said.

There was a wave of mutterings and murmurings from the animals assembled.

'All human beings are the same!' Firebrand shouted. He seemed annoyed that his wife had spoken up for Burt. My family were being hunted by humans and their dogs long before this Hunter came here. We came to Wood-Land because men on horses had killed all of our friends. But we knew the humans would find this place sooner or later. Nowhere in the world is safe from them, but we foxes are survivors. We have even infiltrated their towns, along with the town rats of course.'

'To think they call *us* vermin,' a rat piped up.

'Quite right, and I can tell you this. The rule for survival with humans is simple: if you see them, run away. We survived then and we survive now by avoiding all humans at all costs!'

'Desperate times call for desperate measures, Firebrand, and if this lad speaks the truth and he has killed Wolf, the Kingdom of Wood-Land owes him a debt of gratitude. And there is another matter, of course. In speaking our language, this human has shown himself to be an exception to the rule of man.'

Burt's eyes had adjusted to the dark and he looked around in wonder. There was everything from rabbits and rodents and hedgehogs to deer and badgers and foxes. There was even a snake slithering around beside the mice. Predators and prey stood side by side, united by a common cause.

In the centre, the badger, the emissary, stood resting on his staff.

He noticed an owl's big eyes staring at him from above. *Twit-twoo*, it said, which means hello.

Then Burt gasped. The trees lining the clearing were full of more bird species than he could name. They perched alongside squirrels on branches staring down as if they were in a theatre. He strained his eyes to see if Starling had come.

'And there is the matter of the prophecy,' the badger said. 'Was it not written in the days of old, when all the world was Wood-Land and animals ruled the Earth, that one day a human boy would come who could speak our language? He would be a great warrior who would fight for us and speak on our behalf to his own people, who would deliver us from evil. Was it not said that he would lead us in the fight against those who steal our land and hunt us for sport? Do you remember what the girl said? That when the warrior came the animals would rule, and Mother Earth would be reborn!'

Burt thought he had better put a stop to all of this silliness. 'I promise I don't mean any of you any harm, but I don't know anything about prophecies or the Earth's mummy. I have come to catch the monster who hunts this land because his ghost has haunted my dreams. I've travelled many miles on this quest and now he has my dog Sandy. I must go to fight him, with or without your help.'

'Tell us your story, young man,' the badger said.

'My name is Burt Marshmallow ...' Burt began, and then he told the creatures everything that had happened to him. He told them the story I've been telling you and he spoke long into the night. And it ended with him escaping the fisherman's hut.

The creatures were stunned by his bravery and some were deeply moved. They cried for Sandy and told Burt their own terrible stories about the monster. He had been hunting them for food; chopping down the trees they lived under and using his dog to hound them out of their holes.

'Can anyone speak on behalf of this boy? Can anyone vouch for the truth of his story? Could this be the other Golden Child – the one who is born to lead? The badger seemed to look up at the stars.

'Now just wait a minute. I'm the head of all military operations ...' Firebrand began.

'Silence!' the emissary said. Then from the trees Starling swooped down and whispered in the emissary's ear. They spoke for some time. Burt wanted to talk to her and tell her everything he'd been through. Then, to Burt's surprise, Humperdink the otter came out of nowhere and spoke to the badger as well.

'It seems,' badger finally said, 'this young boy has a history of saving animals. He has already saved the birds' eggs from a fairy and fought a thieving river troll, and he has done a good turn to Mr Otter here – he furnished him with a boat. These are good deeds indeed. And was it not said that the Golden Child would treat animals as equals and with exceptional kindness?'

Burt was rather confused by all this. That's what his mum and dad used to call him: Golden Boy.

The animals all spoke as one and before Burt

82

knew it he had been lifted up over their heads. Then they started chanting excitedly.

'The Saviour has come. The Saviour has come.'

Badger spoke out above the din.

'I call this special convention with the birds and the river folk over, and we thank you for your advice. I hereby declare that things are looking up. This is the boy of the prophecy, the saviour who, it was said, would come at a time of dire need, to save the natural world and lead our people towards a brighter future. We must take him to the king of Wood-Land, Lord Protector of the Creatures of the Ground, to receive his judgement post haste. Let it be said and let it be done.'

A procession of animals set off through the darkness. It felt very strange and squirmy to be carried along by the animals and the long line they formed must have looked like a giant centipede. They took Burt deep into the woods until they reached a great big tree, which Burt thought was marvellous, but instead of climbing up it the animals stopped by a big hole beneath its roots. Then the emissary stepped forwards and took Burt by the hand.

'I would like to welcome you to my humble home.'

12

Badger's Living Room

The badger appeared to be waiting for Burt to enter first, so he got down on his stomach and slithered into the hole. He felt a bit like an earthworm going underground and it was really very cramped. The tunnel wiggled slowly down. It was very dark and the air tasted dirty. But after a time it opened up into a chamber and Burt found a step by the edge that served as a seat.

He couldn't even see his own hand in front of his face. It was like the light of the world had abandoned this place. But if he could have seen he would have known that the delegates from the tribes of Wood-Land were filing in and sitting all about him.

Burt thought about asking for his flashlight back but they had reacted quite badly to that last time, so he rummaged through his things and found the matches he'd used to light the fisherman's stove. He didn't realise he had them but he cautiously struck one to see what was going on by the tiny flickering flame.

The match gave off an eerie orange light and he saw the room was alive with bustling animals of many kinds, too many to count before his fingers got burnt.

Then the emissary spoke.

'Perhaps I can help you see things clearly, Burt.'

He tapped his staff twice and the crystal on top lit up with a bluish nightlight. They appeared to be in some kind of living room, although almost everything in it was carved out of mud. Mud sofas stuck out of the wall and mud stools rose up from the floor.

The walls were tiled with jewels that caught the badger's light and there were rocks with pretty patterns like paintings you could look at. Big flat rocks jutted out like shelves and the badger had placed flowers on top of them. Four big wooden pillars held the ceiling up, making it all look quite grand. Badger explained these were roots from the great tree above.

A big block of mud in the middle served as a table, with a flat rock for a table top. The surface of the table seemed to be moving, which was weird. Then something horrible occurred to Burt. The table was crawling with insects.

'Please do help yourself to refreshments. Can I interest you in a dung beetle, young man? They're in season.'

'Urrgh, no thank you. What is the matter with you animals? You keep eating horrid things.'

'Well,' said the badger in an offended voice, 'I see you haven't got much in the way of manners!'

Many of the other animals came forward and feasted on the buffet.

'Sorry, I didn't mean to be rude, it just happens sometimes.'

'Don't worry, we can dispense with formalities. I'd like us to be friends. You can call me Badger. The badger held his paw out and Burt gave him five.'

'Why are you called Badger? That's like me being called Human.'

'Ah-ha. Good question. I'm called Badger because I am the oldest creature in Wood-Land, which makes me its emissary. It is our tradition for the emissary to take their species name. I used to be called Fred. You have a wonderfully inquisitive mind, you know? You ask lots of questions and that is the very best way to learn.'

'Excuse me, noble squire. May I have a word? I'm afraid we have got off on the wrong foot.' The fox Firebrand approached with his wife Dawn standing behind, cross-armed. 'I want you to know that I accept the emissary's judgement. And if there is any fighting to be done, you will not be on your own. What you witnessed was not a normal meeting. It was a council of war with our allies, the tree and river folk. Our armies are now mobilising. We creatures are experts at tracking and survival in these woods. I would like to offer my personal assistance in any mission you undertake.'

Burt thought it best to just say 'yes'.

'You were not offended by my husband speaking out against you, I hope?' said Dawn. 'He has seen some terrible things and is slow to trust humans.'

'Not at all. Any enemy of the monster is a friend of mine.'

There was a scuffling and a small blind mole emerged from a hole of some kind, which opened up beneath a mantelpiece. The badger went over and whispered something rather longwinded in its ear. Then he gave it an earthworm to eat and sent it on its way, and the tunnel magically closed again.

'What was that?'

'The moles are the king's messengers.'

'Yes, but that hole.'

'Ah, that is a portal. All animal holes are connected, but we enchant them to trick prying human eyes. Our ancestors passed this knowledge down to us from the old times. Back then, we stuck to our animal family tribes and the tunnels weren't connected. Now, however, we have united under one banner. Our numbers were dwindling and we could not survive the attack on Wood-Land if we were fighting among ourselves. So we elected a monarch from our number and they have reigned peacefully over this kingdom ever since.

'You see there is no more hunting among the animals. We mostly live off plants and insects now. Although we also trade fish with the otters and get fruit, nuts and honey from the squirrels, birds and bees.'

'Yes, although I catch those foxes looking at me funny sometimes,' said the nervous rabbit from before, as it munched on a dandelion.

'Nonsense, we love eating spiders,' Dawn said with a sly grin. 'Very filling.'

The mole re-emerged.

'Ahem. May I present His Excellency King George the Great, Lord Protector of Wood-Land and Queen Georgina, Grand Priestess of the Ground on Which We Walk.' The little blind creature then proceeded to play a snail-shell horn rather badly.

With that a ferret emerged sporting a huge red robe and elaborate crown. It was jewel-encrusted and looked a bit like a big human ring. Alongside him a mink with fabulous white fur walked with her nose held high in the air. They looked a bit like puppets the way they pranced along the ground.

All of the creatures had stood as they entered and now bowed very low.

'Hello,' said Burt.

'Is this the boy? Are you quite sure, Badger,' said the ferret king.

'A bit scruffy, isn't it?' the slender mink agreed.

'I am quite sure, Your Highness, but there is of course the test.'

'What test?' Burt's heart sank. He hated tests.

'It is said,' badger intoned, turning to him, 'that the chosen one would be able to enter the Underworld and return and climb the great tree that towers above us, and speak with it, for the tree would be his very own. It is no easy task and highly dangerous. But if you choose to go, Burt, you will emerge as a grown-up – if not in body then in mind. You will have proved yourself worthy to lead us.'

'My husband speaks of the good and evil that

88

exist in your people, human beings,' the queen chirped in.

Burt looked at her crestfallen.

'Yes, I'm afraid so, Burt,' Badger said sadly. 'People have lost their way. If I may explain, Sire?'

'Of course, Badger.'

'You see in the olden days the whole world was wild. It was covered in woodland as ancient as the rocks and it was teaming with life. At first, humans lived as part of that natural world because humans were a type of animal to begin with and they formed a special friendship with the trees. Back then people lived with their families, which were called tribes. They spoke with the animals and looked after the wild world under the guidance of the trees, which connected them with the Earth.

'The problem was that people grew less connected with the world. And when they stopped talking to the trees, the trees couldn't talk to them. They learned how to make tools with their hands like axes and they chopped the trees down so that they could farm the land instead. At first there was enough space to go around but because they could grow as much food as they liked, more and more people were born and they started building cities and clearing more and more of the woodland away, until today it is almost gone.

'The city people started to speak a different language to the animals entirely and they began to fight among themselves. They learned how to make weapons for waging war and they fought over who owned what bits of the world. That's when the evil got into humankind. Their selfishness and greed grew and many people hurt one another until a new evil emerged – creatures who enjoyed hurting people.

'The mother of the world, Mother Earth, who nurtured the life of every living thing, grew cross at all this and she summoned the animals and wild people. It is said that Mother Earth rose out of a lake as a beautiful woman with a child in her belly. She told those assembled that city-dwellers would make better and better tools and weapons and that they would use them to take everything they wanted from the world because it was in their nature and they didn't think of the future. The old knowledge would be lost and there was nothing they could do because she was being overrun.

'She told the leaders of the animal tribes that she would surely die. The dominion of man could not last forever because they would take the world to the brink of destruction. People have to learn their lesson: they can't take whatever they want and they would have to learn to share. The animals' task has been to survive and guard the secret. Many tribes did not but the secret survived and it was this:

'The only hope for the future lies with the children of the world. The children of humanity can still learn to heal the world and save the wild. In the days of old, Mother Earth knew this day would come. She summoned the leaders of the wild people and from the best in them she made a child, a boy who could one day be born to lead his people away from catastrophe. And within herself she conceived the world's rebirth, a baby girl who would bring grace and love. The boy and girl were to be the Golden Children, born to save the world from man's abuse.

'And so it is, now humankind's selfishness and greed have taken their toll and they have realised that the world is out of their control, Mother Earth has given us the gift of hope in the form of two children. It was said they would be able to communicate with animals and change physical form and they would find each other and receive love's blessing, by swimming in the lake where her spirit dwelled.'

As Badger finished his tale, he looked Burt squarely in the eyes.

'Burt, we believe the boy is you.'

'I don't understand.'

'Burt, there are some tasks you must fulfil before this will make sense to you. They are very dangerous, but if you *are* indeed the Golden Child, you have come to us in the nick of time to save Wood-land.'

'What do I have to do?'

'The Hunter we call Hades seeks to plunge the world into eternal darkness. He is the enemy of Mother Earth and plots her destruction and that of everything she does. Mother Earth looks after the animals in the natural world and places her hope in the children of the world to find a way to live in harmony and peace with their environment. Hades, meanwhile, speaks to the evil in people.

Their greed and selfishness he uses to make them take more than the world can sustain, and when people hurt others they come to serve him ...'

'Then we have to stop him,' Burt interrupted.

'Your path is known from the prophecy. You must cross the Eternal River and enter the labyrinth of destiny to decide your fate. There you will have to face Hades and his minions in the land of the dead but help will be at hand. I will be watching over you up here. I can see you in my crystal ball.'

Badger's staff glowed brightly and Burt was shocked to see his face appear under his paw.

'I will guide you to the Chamber of Truth, where you must recover the Sword of Justice to aid you in your fight. All I can tell you now is that only he who does not fear death will return from this quest. But return you shall, of that I am convinced.

'Then you will find what you seek, Burt. When you return you must climb the great tree and it will help you in the second stage of your quest, for it is guardian of the Shield of Human Kindness, of which little is known except that it comes from the heavens above. It is said no evil can penetrate it.

'Finally, you must learn to navigate the sky at night and follow your lucky stars to the Lake of Prophecy. If the Lady of the Lake gives you her love, you will gain your armour and the blessing of this court. It is said no evil can hide from he who wears that suit, nor hurt the one that wears it.'

The queen looked at Burt carefully. 'Do you have the courage to fulfil these tasks, young man?'

'Yes,' Burt said. 'I'll do it.'

'Your Highnesses, if I may …' Firebrand the fox cut in. The king and queen nodded. 'A delegation of animals will meet you there, Burt, and ride with you to the mountain caves when you pass these tests. But I warn you, the greatest task of all will be the fight for the natural world. And if we are to triumph in that, we will need everyone to help. So in the meantime we will muster our army and prepare.'

'Very well, it is agreed. Let it be said and let it be done,' said the King regally. 'Now, human boy, come and bow before me.'

Burt bowed low.

'Do you agree to fight on behalf of the animals of the Kingdom of Wood-Land?'

'I do.'

'And do you pledge allegiance to your king and faithfully promise to do whatever you are told?'

Burt hesitated. Then Badger kicked him.

'Ow, yeah OK.'

The king drew a sword from beneath his robes and tapped him on both shoulders.

'You are hereby appointed Knight of the Kingdom of Wood-Land. Then he leant forward and whispered: 'Just make sure you don't get any ideas, chosen one! There can only be one king.' Then out loud he added: 'I'm afraid you must do the first part on your own, Burt. If you do not wish to continue, then we will all understand.'

'Of course I wish to continue. I need to save Sandy and I can't find her and save her without help. Just tell me which way to go.'

'Enter the tunnel before you,' said Badger, 'and it will take you to the Underworld. There you must confront your worst fears and thereby free your soul. You will find your way in there. I have every faith in you, Burt,'

'We will see you at the lake,' said Firebrand. 'Good luck, brave Sir Burt!'

'And remember, Sir Burt,' said Badger, 'in order to grow up you must first know yourself. It isn't your age that makes you an adult!'

The tunnel opened up until it was a boy-sized hole. It looked like quite a steep slide.

'Well, here goes!' he said to no one in particular. Then he took a deep breath and jumped in.

13

The Underworld

Burt slid down a dusty tunnel as if he were on a water slide. The earth moved freely beneath him speeding him along and the dusty air choked him and stung his eyes. Deeper and deeper he slid until the air around him grew hot. Burt thought he was about to suffocate when finally the sloping tunnel petered out and levelled off into an underground cave, where Burt came to rest.

He got up and brushed himself down. He could see slimy wet walls either side of him and above him spiky rocks stuck out of a ceiling above his head. Ahead there was a foggy green light and he could hear the sound of running water. He went forward to investigate and quickly came upon an underground river.

Burt looked first one way then the other. The river flowed round a bend from the left and ran off into the distance. There was no way to walk along the bank – the tunnel had no edges. That's when he noticed a boat sitting beside a hole in the bank on the opposite side. Maybe someone was nearby.

'Hello!' he called. 'Is anyone there?'

'Hello?'

He heard a spluttering cough echo out of the hole.

'Huh huh-huh, what? Who's that come a visiting? What's that racket?'

A river rat poked its head out of the hole and peered towards him groggily.

'Hmmm. Don't look very dead to me. That's strange. Better have a closer look.'

It clambered into the boat and started rowing itself across the river until it landed close to where Burt was standing.

'You dead?'

'No, I'm not.'

'Why not? Supposed to be only dead people comes to the Underworld. Who are you?'

'My name's Burt Marshmallow. I've come to find my ancestors and learn my fate.'

'OK, what have you got to pay for your passage?'

Burt thought about this. He had all his things with him but no money at all.

'What do you want? I have some food, a rain coat, erm ...'

'A raincoat? That's a lot of use down here. Don't think it'll fit me somehow anyway.'

'Um ...' Burt was stumped.

'I want information. What business do you have coming down here? There's no way back, you know?'

'*I* can get back. Badger said I'd return.'

'Badger? … Oh! Are you the one they call Golden Child?'

'Yes.'

'Oh! Well, sshh … You'd better keep your voice down then.'

'Do you know where Hades hides in the Underworld?' Burt thought this rat was rather odd but it seemed to know a lot.

'Oh, Hades doesn't *hide* down here; on the surface maybe, but not down here. Down here he's king. And he won't like you dropping in one little bit. Unarmed as well – you're mad!'

'I'm looking for the Chamber of Truth,' Burt said nervously. This was sounding dangerous. 'I've got a catapult.'

'Um, oh. Oh, well then. I'll tell you what. Let me help you out. What Badger says goes, even down here. All I want in return is a lock of your golden hair.'

The rat took a knife from its belt and cut some of Burt's hair off.

'There. If you survive this, you must be the luckiest boy in the world and no mistake. This will be my good-luck charm.'

Finally they set off and on the other side the rat offered some further assistance.

'Here, come in here. You don't want to go on the other side, where all the dead things are. Just come in my hole where it's safe and sound and I'll take you as far as I can underground. You could say it's a short cut.'

A short cut to what? Burt thought.

Burt squeezed into the rat's hole, which magically grew, and crawled down the tunnel until he reached an exit.

'Up here and out. You'll have to brave it now, brave boy. Watch out, cos Hades is about, but we skipped the worst of it.'

'Wait! Badger said to remember that ... you can't grow up until you know yourself. What does that mean?'

'Oh yeah, he set me free down here, you know. He asked me to find something out, said, what was it? ... "What is there to be afraid of?"'

Burt thanked the rat and poked his head out into what looked like a graveyard, only there was no church in sight. He crawled out sheepishly into the chill air. Wherever he was, it looked like the Earth's surface at night, except without any stars or moon to bring their light. Instead, there was just what looked like thunder clouds above as far as the eye could see, and an eerie mist blanketing the ground.

Burt walked along between mounds of earth and the gravestones sticking up. They were everywhere. Up ahead he saw a path and decided to head towards it. No sooner had he set foot on it than a low rumbling growl sent a terrible shiver through every bone in his body. All he could see were some eyes, six, staring straight at him. This was where Burt discovered what fear really is. This was where Burt discovered his fear of death.

Suddenly the sky flashed with lightning and lit up everything with a fiery light. And there stood Wolf growling high on a mound. Death had changed Wolf for the worse, because he now had three slathering, snarling heads.

'It's you. I know you!' the heads cried in unison.

Burt sprang into action, whipping out his catapult and firing a hail of stones at the hellish hound, but it just shook its heads and snapped at them as if they were little flies, crushing them in its multiple jaws. Realising his catapult was useless, Burt began to run as fast as his legs would carry him. His mind was racing faster than it ever had but it just made his body feel slow and clumsy. He called out to Sandy but of course she couldn't come. He was on his own now.

'Your dog Sandy can't help you now. Not down here!'

'No, no.'

The different heads spoke. 'Trick us, kill us, will you? We'll see what we can do with you. This is where we live now. Master will be interested to know who's here.'

Burt remembered the monster he couldn't escape in his nightmares. He knew he couldn't escape this creature; he just knew he wouldn't get away like this. It was gaining on him all the time and he was going round in circles trying to escape, dodging round gravestones, darting this way and that. Eventually he could run no more and he bent double gasping for air. With the last of his strength he grabbed a hold of a gravestone and cowered behind it, hoping Wolf had lost sight of him. Then ... silence.

This place was strange. It didn't feel real. It felt

like a scary story or a nightmare in his head. Perhaps all that mattered was what was in his mind. He stood up and felt a shudder pass through him. The dog had disappeared.

This was his test, Burt decided. He was facing his fears. What he didn't realise, though, was that Wolf had been called off by his master. And now his voice came booming across the graveyard:

'Burt Marshmallow, you escaped me once but time has told its tales on you. You join me now in the Land of Death. It rather spoils the job of killing you, which I was oh-so-looking-forward to.'

Burt could see him now. The one he'd known as the fisherman. Hades had an awful pointy face: it was a face like Flutterby's and it had big ears like wings. And his eyes ... his eyes burned with a fire, fuelled by his monstrous desire. His mouth had sharp animal's teeth and a long black tongue, which licked his lips. He drew a sword from his black robe and as he held it aloft it fired lightning far into the sky.

'I am the outside world's destruction, little boy. I am the Lord of the Underworld and today is your Day of Judgement. No one returns from this place, this is my domain. Now you will join my army of the damned.'

Hades started to approach him and Burt began to walk backwards.

'I'll never do anything you tell me – I'd rather die.'

'Oh, I'm afraid you already have, to all intents and purposes.'

'Well, then I have nothing to fear from you, do I?'

'You do fear pain, do you not? Every evil mind that ever lived is at my beck and call. They will visit destruction upon your body and mind and cast your ruin aside.'

All around Burt the earth opened up, and all of the people buried in the Underworld started digging themselves out of their graves.

'Do you really think a little boy could challenge me?'

Squalid decaying skeletons were pulling themselves loose and surrounding him. Burt became rooted to the spot. But he didn't panic. He stood stock-still and thought.

So where am I? The land of the dead. Well, I'm alive. Can the living be killed by the dead?

Hades and his army seemed to freeze.

'Little boy, I am fear. I am your fear. You are trapped here with me for ever. This fear will overcome you. It will blind you.'

'No!' Burt said. 'I'm in charge in my head and that puts me in charge of my fear. I decide what I'm afraid of. If I feel myself getting afraid, I just have to think of something else.'

'That's right, Burt,' Badger's voice seemed to sound from the sky. 'Hades is lord of the dead, not the living. He is master of the evil, not the good. It is only fear that gives him the power to harm you.'

Burt forced himself to think of something nice, which is a very hard thing to do when you're afraid. He closed his eyes and he concentrated with all his might and he thought of his garden on a lovely, sunny day. He opened his eyes again and the mists were swirling around and around. Hades stood frozen and confused. There was something wrong with him. He couldn't move.

Burt laughed. The shoe's on the other foot now. He feeds on fear down here. If I'm not scared of him, there's nothing he can do.

He smiled a big wide smile and the mist seemed to lift, revealing a wide chamber about him. Instead of thunder clouds, the ceiling solidified into jutting rocks which dripped water and showed pretty marbled colours. He was in an underground cave again, dotted with rocks. Those were the gravestones he had thought he had seen. What was going on?

He thought about what the rat had said. What is there to be afraid of? I have to work out what makes me scared so that I won't get scared anymore, then I'll be safe. Hmmm.

Sticks and stones may break my bones but words will never hurt me, he thought to himself. I'm scared of getting hurt, but if I'm not scared, nothing can hurt me. But what if I do get scared, then maybe it can, oh no, what if…

Burt stopped himself thinking. He hadn't been hurt at all, not in here at least. And anyway, he'd been hurt before and he'd got better. Then he heard Badger's voice echo inside him:

'Burt, you don't have to do this alone. Let me help you make sense of it inside. I am in your heart and in your mind.'

102

'Those things,' Burt replied in his head, 'that just happened were like my nightmares, weren't they? They're my fears that I feel inside.'

'Something like that, Burt. You are in the Underworld and there is evil in that place, but it can only get to you if you let it. You must have a strong mind to do what you've done – to escape the fear that Hades commands. In here it is your fear of being afraid that will be your nemesis, so you must keep thinking. When do you feel fear?'

'I get scared when its dark and I see shadows or hear funny noises and I'm on my own.'

'You are scared of being alone in the dark?'

'I'm scared of things that might be *in the dark*.'

'If you're scared and there's nothing there, then you're afraid of nothing ... but it happens anyway, doesn't it?

'I *imagine* things are there.'

'So you are scared of your own imagination. You have an over-active imagination, Burt. Hades would use your imagination against you if you let him.'

'So what can I do?'

'Just dream instead. Think happy thoughts.'

Burt was relieved. He could do that.

'You have faced your fears, but that does not mean they will disappear. You just have to let yourself feel the way you feel and understand why you feel that way. Then you can gain control of it and use it to see the truth in yourself ...' Badger's voice faded.

Burt stared at nothing for a second. He felt like his brain had melted.

'This is getting weird. I'd better be off, but which way should I go?' he said out loud to himself.

14

The Labyrinth

Burt walked on and found a large cave opening. He had a feeling this was the right way to go, although he had no idea why. The tunnel circled and zigzagged and climbed slowly upwards until eventually the walls changed. They looked to be made of stone bricks now, and candles – there were candles burning on the wall! Where was he now? It looked like the deepest dungeons of a castle of some kind.

He started to explore the strange stone passages. This place was huge and he found himself going round in circles. All he could find were corridors. And no matter where he went, through doors, upstairs, downstairs, it all looked much the same. After wandering like this for a while he realised he was in a maze of some kind and he needed to work his way out. This was the Labyrinth.

He looked around and noticed a picture with him in it on the wall. He walked over and had a closer look. It was a painting of the time he and his family had gone to collect Sandy. Burt was cuddling her and feeling her lovely soft fur for the first time. He smiled the same smile he had on in the picture. Then he moved along to another picture beside it. It was of the first time he'd walked Sandy with his dad.

The pictures looked like he had made them himself; he understood everything in them. There were drawings and collages telling stories and family photographs that recorded important moments. They were all over the place now he came to think about it. On walls and ledges. And Burt realised something. These weren't just pictures; these were his memories.

Burt thought about what Badger would say, but he couldn't hear his voice anymore. He knew he had to try to understand his memories to get out of here. Well, where better to start than the beginning. He sought out his earliest memory and then followed the story of his life from the beginning to the present day, and as he thought about all the things he'd done and the people he knew, he seemed to get better and better at finding his way around.

At the end of the trail of pictures Burt came to a door with his name on it. He turned the handle and discovered a room full of all of the things he owned, and all of the interesting things he'd ever discovered. And books, there were shelves full of books that contained all the stories he had ever read or heard. And as he was riffling along the bookshelves and making a mess he found a whole section of books with his name on them.

Everything he'd thought of was written down in them and everything he'd imagined as well, like the games he'd invented. These were things he'd made up using his imagination. He realised he could use this. It contained all his ideas on how to deal with trouble and how to have fun and make things better.

Then Burt wondered where his dreams and wishes came from. And that's when he found a hidden door, which he could have sworn hadn't been there before. It led into a round room that seemed to be made of glass at first sight and had a big fire burning brightly in the middle.

This room was unbelievable. A big dome shone far above, covered in crystals and jewels. The weird thing was that the dome sparkled and changed constantly. In fact, light and colours danced everywhere like a firework display in the middle of the day. Then the lights started to form into lots of images, bits of people and things swimming around him like fishes, but too blurry to quite make out. It was as if there were lots of joined-up television screens all around him. And as he concentrated he discovered he could control what they showed.

I wonder what an alien from Mars would look like, he thought. Then he saw lots of googly eyes and hodgepodge pieces of things merge together into a funny-looking alien. Its eyes were on the end of worms that wriggled about like hair on top of a potato-shaped head, on the front of which was a beak like a bird. Its head wobbled about on top of a body like a bunch of bananas scuttling across the ground like a crab. It was the weirdest thing Burt had ever come up with. Then it started to flicker and everything sort of disappeared as if he were in a drawing, and everything around him had been rubbed out.

This place was something called an 'imaginarium', which is a place where you make stuff up. Of course, the first thing you have to make up is the room itself. This one was wired into Burt's dreams and all the things he dreamed about swam around him like shoals of fish at the aquarium. No wonder – Burt had an overactive imagination.

As he practised, Burt got better and better at controlling the things he saw. He found that he had to feel them because each feeling had a matching thought and that thought made an image appear. He discovered that he could relive all the memories in his memory bank or he could imagine things that could happen to him or someone else. And when he thought about the future it seemed strangely believable; like he was finding things out that he couldn't possibly know.

Where am I now? he thought.

'This is the Chamber of Truth, Burt,' a voice from the fire said. He had ignored the fire completely until now. But as he concentrated on it the room took shape around him, making walls and a ceiling and furniture. Before he knew it, he was standing in some kind of dinner hall fit for a king to banquet in and Burt walked over to the fire marvelling. It stood ablaze in a great column of flames. And in the flames a face appeared. It looked like an old man and it spoke to Burt very lovingly.

'We are in the timeless space of your soul, Burt; where your dreams were born and your destiny is known. In here, you can find out anything you like about your future. It will tell you all you need to know. '

'Who are you?'

'I am you when all is said and done. I am you when you are whole.'

'Eh?'

'I am your future.'

'When I'm a grown up?'

'Yes.'

'Why didn't you say that then? This place is cool. Can it be anything I can imagine?'

'Yes, you can live out your dreams in here. Tell me, would you like to stay for ever?'

Burt had to think about this for a moment. 'No, I need to get out and save Sandy. And then I have to go home.'

'Good boy,' the voice said. 'Let me do something for you now. Let me answer your prayers.'

The face disappeared and the fire grew and flared up into a tunnel shape. Then there was a snap and wishing well appeared in its place, with a stone base. Burt went over and peered deep into the well's waters. His reflection shimmered thoughtfully on the surface. He thought about what he wished for most in the whole world.

Sandy. He wanted Sandy to be safe. He couldn't forget about Sandy being trapped but he was so frightened of that awful fisherman Hades. His tears rippled the water.

'I just want Sandy to be safe and sound, and to get Hades so he can't hurt anyone else. I'm afraid his evil is getting stronger and will destroy the whole natural world. So I need all of the help I can get, please.'

The water rippled and the face from the fire reappeared in the water. 'That was the very best wish you could have made, Burt. You are a very good boy. If you ever need help, all you have to do is ask.' The face looked thoughtful for a second.

'The age of your innocence is at an end, Burt. Now that you know evil, you have uncovered the good and the strength in yourself, and that means you've come of age. You see, to grow up you needed to understand who you are and what you can do. You had to discover the truth in yourself.

'You must listen to me now: the thing that evil fears most is the truth, because all evil hides from itself. However, when the truth is told, justice must be done.

'Bad people are always starting fights. Now it's time for the good to fight back. The world needs a hero, Burt; someone to give it justice. If you are brave enough to do your best to help others; if you are willing to put yourself in danger, then reach into the wishing well.'

Burt reached into the wishing well and he felt

110

his hand grip something. He drew out a shining silver sword and held it above his head.

'Make your vow.'

Burt felt he knew what to say. 'Whenever a baddy hurts someone I will find out the truth and make it right.'

Now a jewel-studded sheath for the sword gleamed just beneath the surface of the water, This Burt quickly drew out and fastened to his belt.

'That is the Sword of Justice, Burt, and only the righteous can yield it. By pulling it out you have chosen your path and shown yourself to be worthy. You will find it is stronger than any weapon, just as long as your courage holds.'

But you must remember: that sword carries a grave responsibility. You must always be on hand and be sure to use it wisely. You will seek out evil for the rest of your life but you must always stay good and be honest with yourself ...'

With that the room started to shimmer and flicker like one big fire blazing all around, then it started to melt and whirl around him and Burt was worried he'd done something wrong. Then everything seemed to turn into water. It was like someone had pulled the plug out of the bath and it was draining away around him. Then he understood and he jumped into the wishing well.

15

Burt Catches a Rainbow

What happened next felt a bit like being flushed down the toilet. He fell in a rush of water down a slippery tube that swung this way and that until he shot out of a hole into a fast-running stream. This was the river he'd crossed, except now it was moving quickly. Burt realised why too late ... it was approaching a waterfall!

Oh well, let's see where this goes, Burt thought as he was swept over the edge.

Burt fell upside down so all the blood rushed to his head. Then he plunged into a deep underground pool and sank. He didn't stop sinking until he'd hit the rocky bottom because the silver sword he carried was weighing him down. It was a good job that Burt had learned to swim so well because he couldn't very well leave the sword behind now.

He pushed off the bottom of the pool and swam as hard as he could towards the surface. And although his lungs felt as if they were about to burst, he kept holding his breath and kicking. Just in time he felt the water break and he gasped and air rushed into his lungs so hard that he thought he might choke on it. He splashed and spluttered and the relief that he'd made it washed over him. Then he looked around to see where he was now.

He was in an underground lake in a chamber of some kind, but there was no light down here so he couldn't make much out. He was kicking so hard to stay afloat his legs soon started to ache, as if he were peddling up a steep hill on his bike. He guessed a direction and swam until he bumped his head on a wall and he felt his way around the edge in an effort to find an exit. But there was nothing; just stone and some slimy roots hanging down.

Hold on! These roots could be his lifeline. Trees drink from water underground using their roots like elephant trunks. And the water gets sucked all the way to the treetops.

So Burt grabbed a hold and found that the roots were all entangled and clung to the wall of the underground chamber, forming a natural ladder for him to climb.

Burt climbed until he reached the ceiling, where he found the roots had cut through the soil and rock above. *Well, if they can cut through, so can I,* he thought. And where there're roots this deep there must be a great tree above. Perhaps this is the tree I was meant to find.

So Burt unsheathed his sword and discovered something new: it's possible to dig your way up as well as down! And being careful not to damage the roots he followed them to the surface.

Can you guess where he came out?

He came out through badger's living-room floor; almost exactly where he'd come from. How did that happen?

Badger was sitting alone, chewing thoughtfully on an earthworm. He leapt up in shock when he saw Burt's silver sword stick up through the floor near one of his wooden pillars. Then he heard a muffled call and he scrambled to help Burt free, thinking it was lucky he hadn't come up underneath his seat and spiked his bottom.

'I knew you would make it, my dear boy. I could feel it in my bones. You have made an awful mess of my living room though. Never mind.'

Burt drank some water and ate some food from his rucksack, but he was in a hurry to get going. He wanted some fresh air and had to soldier on. But Badger insisted he have a wash first because he was filthy.

'I don't want a bath. These roots lead to my tree, I know it. I have to keep climbing up!'

'You are having a bath. We can't allow the Golden Boy to walk around covered in mud.'

'If I'm the Golden Boy, you can't tell me what to do,' said Burt rather peevishly.

'I can and I am, young man. I am the emissary of Wood-Land and that is precisely my job. And you're obviously tired, too, so you can have a nap after that in the cubs' room.'

Burt gave in eventually. He could do with a rest, it was true.

When he awoke he was fresh as a daisy and Badger gave him one final piece of advice.

'You must follow your heart as you follow a rainbow, Burt. The treasure is always one step ahead. I can't help you this time but there is someone who can. You will know who it is when you find them.'

Burt climbed out of the hole, and immediately above him a great tree grew. He knew at once this was the tree he must climb. He had known as soon as he'd seen it. It was easily the tallest one around and he had already climbed it underground.

The way the branches twisted round made it look like a spiral staircase to the sky. But there were no low-lying branches to grab and the trunk was too thick to shimmy up. Burt couldn't see how he could climb it, so he paused for a moment until the answer came to him.

Then he remembered the rope he had taken from the fisherman's hut. He tied a loop in the end and swung it above his head. After a few attempts he managed to catch it on a thick enough branch, high up on one side. Then he pulled himself up until he reached the first branch.

He climbed and swung about like a monkey having fun and pretty soon he was higher than all the other trees and he could see for miles and miles, including the mountains where he knew Sandy must be.

'Have you finished having fun yet, because there's work to do, you know?'

'Who was that?' Burt was getting so used to these surprises he almost expected them now.

'Well, are you going to answer me or not, young man?'

'Badger?'

'Oh you've met young Badger, have you? Delightful fellow: I've been watching over his family for many generations, you know.'

'Who are you?'

'My name is Buddy and you're Burt, I believe.'

'How do you know my name?'

'Because I've been expecting you, of course.'

Burt couldn't see another living creature anywhere but the voice sounded like it was right beside him. Who the bloomin' 'eck was it?

'Where are you? Stop hiding – I want to see your face.'

'Well, you're a fine one to talk. I thought you'd never get here.'

'Why were you expecting me to get here?'

'Because I'm your tree, you imbecile! What a silly question!'

Burt would have toppled backwards off the branch he was sitting on if it hadn't suddenly grabbed a hold of him like a great big hand. And now instead of climbing, the branches passed him up, until he was sitting on a stubby branch in front of two big droopy eyes. Burt could see love in these eyes, so he calmed right down.

'You've been talking to other trees. Why didn't you think to talk to me?'

'I ... I don't know. Am I dreaming again?'

'No, of course you're not dreaming and this isn't make-believe. You're growing up far too fast, if you

116

ask me. You're already starting to disbelieve the magic that's right in front of your eyes.'

'I want to grow up so I can fight the monster.'

'You could fight monsters in your sleep, Burt. You've been doing it all your life. But growing up is a serious thing. You can't ever have fun like a kid again.'

'I was having fun climbing until you interrupted.'

'Oh yes, well, that's different. You do have to go and help Sandy and we're in a bit of a hurry cos I've got something to show you. You could call it a present, I suppose.'

'Wait, how do you know so much about me?'

'Another silly question, although I suppose you're not to know yet. You see, I know everything that you know because you are a part of me. The major disadvantage of being a tree is that you can't move around, which is why we have you curious creatures to go around and find new things out for us. The sad thing is that most people never even meet their tree, or believe it exists, which is a tragedy.

'We watch over you all your lives. We see the world through your young eyes. And your feelings flow through us like water so we know exactly how you feel all of the time.'

'You see everything that I do? So are you like my memory.'

Ah, that's a better question, but no, not quite. Your mind and my mind are one but I have the benefit of experience, so I see much more than you

117

do. And I can speak to you even when you're by yourself, *if* you listen very carefully.'

'Whoa ... are you my very own tree then or do you watch over other creatures as well?'

No, every human child has their very own tree assigned by Mother Earth, although tragically grown-ups often chop them down. But a little piece of everyone you know and love lives in me as well, so I keep an eye on them, too. And the trees in this wood are all our friends and family.'

'Wow, I'm going to have a lot of friends.'

Buddy showed Burt all of the trees in Wood-Land, including his daddy's, which grew on a hill in the distance. Apparently, trees only got talkative when they'd been found by their very own child.

'What about my family tree?'

'That was your great, great-granddad's tree all right. It's a great shame when a tree gets chopped down, but it's an even greater shame when a person gets chopped down and the tree lives on. That foolish war took a lot of lives. The Great War the grown-ups called it back then.'

'The animals are talking about war now.'

'Yes, well, you will need to learn to help them, Burt, or I'm afraid Wood-Land is doomed. You have been so unlucky with all the horrid things you've faced but, as they say, what doesn't kill you makes you stronger. It's because you never give up that I grew so tall, and we got this splendid view. I've been waiting to meet you for an awfully long time; long before you were even born.'

'You mean you knew the prophecy?'

'I am the prophecy and so are you. Mother Earth made us both.'

'Can I see your face properly? The tree's eyes looked strong as if they were burning with the fire he had found underground. But Burt felt a little odd just talking to two big eyes. He needed to be held back because the face was so big he couldn't see it all. And, in actual fact, what he was sat on was the big tree's nose.'

'Oh yes, of course. How silly of me.'

Two great branches swung in from either side and gripped Burt before holding him out in front of the tree in mid-air.

Wow, his tree was pretty ugly. It had a nose that looked a bit like it was upside down. It was quite long and it pointed up and out and a bit to one side. Its mouth was rather crooked and it had funny sticky-out lips like a beak. Nevertheless, it had a nice wide smile and its bright eyes smiled as well.

'You look very nice. Pleased to meet you, Buddy.'

'Why, thank you, Master Burt; it's a pleasure to have you on board at last. Now, can I show you something? Like I said, there's little time to waste.'

Burt was passed up higher and higher until he noticed a layer of cloud up above. Then somewhere in there, where he couldn't see much, he was set down on something that wasn't a branch. It was the floor of ... of a tree house!

'Ah, thank you, Buddy!' he shouted as he jumped and danced about.

Well, this tree house wasn't like a bird box or a

nest; this was more like a wooden fort. It was wrapped all the way around the tree with the trunk growing through the middle like a great big pillar. And it had four different rooms with towers on the corners, where you could climb up some stairs and look out and fire your catapult. This was even better than he could have imagined.

He was sitting on one of the battlements thinking about how cool this was and looking out above the clouds and into a different world. What he saw was a landscape of dark and light clouds of all different shapes and sizes. And in contrast to the Underworld, the whole world seemed to shine with light.

He looked out on the islands of milky-white clouds floating in a bright blue sky, and on the wispy trails like the froth of waves that caught the light and glowed. Through the gaps light shone in beams and lit up the world beneath, which was a beautiful fresh shade of green. He could see the whole of Wood-Land when the clouds parted, as if it were just a little mossy lawn and the mountains beyond just a rockery.

Dotted around and up above were stray storm clouds, standing out sharp like shadows in the light. Burt thought they just seemed to add to the beauty, to the shades and textures in his ever-changing view. And, after all, they did water the plants. But there was something strangely menacing about them. As if they could grow and swallow the beautiful sky. As if to prove the point, a raincloud burst above him and drenched his clothes. It passed quite quickly and an eerie mist descended on the clouds, only for a glorious rainbow to appear in its wake.

'Hello, Burt. I thought you might be getting lonely up here on your own.'

Burt spun around smiling. 'Hello, Starling, how did you find me up here?'

'Well, you do rather stick out like a great big sore thumb.'

'Well, how did you know I'd be in here?'

'Because I know Buddy, of course. He's friends with my tree. And anyway, Badger told me you made it here. The creatures are having a big party down there to celebrate.'

'Oh. Have you seen how beautiful the clouds look from here?'

'I know – I love to fly with the clouds. I wish you could come with me some time. It's a bit like being a part of a great work of art, full of all the light and textures and colours of your heart. Just look at that beautiful rainbow.'

'It's amazing, isn't it? Do you know that a rainbow is made out of sunlight that breaks up in the rain? And everyone sees their own rainbow, because it depends on where you see it from.'

'I think that's your rainbow right there.'

'Hmmm. Yeah I think so too. Do you think there's treasure at the end?'

'Why don't we go and see.'

'Don't be daft – you can't catch a rainbow. I've tried before. And anyway I can't walk on clouds; I'd sink and fall. Badger said chasing a rainbow was like following your heart or something. I think he means you never quite get everything you want.'

'No, he said you must follow your heart like you follow a rainbow, as in if you keep going there's always more to find. He once told me the journey is more important than the destination in life.'

'I wish I could catch a rainbow though. I'd use it to make a scarf for Buddy. But when you run after a rainbow it always stays the same distance away.'

'You don't catch a rainbow by running, you muppet; you have to learn how to fly.'

'I don't know if you've noticed but I am a human being. I don't have wings, only arms and ...' Then Burt remembered something. 'I think I need the treasure at the end of that rainbow to help Sandy. And Badger said he couldn't help me but there is someone who can. I think that someone is *you*: can you teach me how to fly?'

Starling laughed a happy laugh. 'Of course I can. All you had to do was ask. But first you have to give me a kiss.

This bird was doing his head in. What was she going on about? But she insisted and she gave him a little peck on the cheek. And he gave her a peck back ... a real peck. He had a beak! And he'd shrunk. Burt had turned into a little bird, fluttering in thin air!

'What? Who? How?' He perched on the side of his tree-house turret.

'Don't worry, don't worry. I knew you could do it. Sorry I tricked you like that. When you give someone a kiss, it tells them how you're feeling.

And sometimes it makes them feel like you. I feel like a bird that can fly and now by magic, so do you! *Voilà!*

'What am I?'

'You've turned into a magpie. They're a bird well known for seeking treasure.'

Burt looked himself over then fluttered into the air again. *He could actually fly.*

'Wow! This is an even cooler present than my tree house.' Burt was getting the hang of this. 'Let's go!'

He didn't even bother worrying about what to do, he just jumped off the edge and flew off with Starling swooping and whooping by his side. 'This is so fun! I always wanted to fly!'

'Yeah, I know; it's my favourite thing in the world.'

Burt flew down and said goodbye to Buddy.

'Don't worry, I'm watching. Just remember if you grow up too fast, you'll miss out on all the fun.'

'Don't worry, I won't.'

Flying is the most amazing feeling it is possible to have. They swooped and dived and spun and their insides seemed to leap around in the opposite direction. Burt felt light-headed and giddy and excited and he was so happy that Starling was there to share all the fun with him.

'Look at the clouds, Starling! Have you ever seen anything like it? It's like a dream world or something. Is this what heaven looks like?'

Starling opened her beak and fluffed up her feathers. He guessed that was how birds smile.

'Should we go and look at your rainbow?' she called.

'Yeah, OK, can we really get close?'

'Get close? We can walk on it, well, hop. I'm afraid birds aren't very good at walking.'

Up close, the rainbow looked like a multi-coloured, humpbacked bridge, stretching between the dark clouds and the light. Starling landed first on the green streak and Burt set down on the blue.

'C'mon,' she called, hopping along and laughing.

Burt raced as fast as he could to the other side, hopping clumsily along like a sack race on sports day. But he didn't seem to get anywhere. Meanwhile Starling hopped from side to side and all the colours lit up and made a musical sound as she bounced on them. Then she sang:

> Rainbows made of sunlight
> Drawbridges in the rain
> If you catch a rainbow and know its secret
> Then the greatest treasure you will claim.

'You have to speak the secret colour code and the treasure is yours,' Starling went on. 'Do you know what it is? Richard Of York Gave Battle In Vain. That's the rainbow colour code.'

A bubble seemed to form around them and they floated now through the coloured light. The front of their bubble grew white hot in the sun's gaze and they drifted to the other side glowing brighter and brighter. When they hit the end the light focused and flashed and they threw their wings up and closed their eyes because it was too bright to look at. It formed a dome in front of them that filtered the light and when they opened their eyes again and recovered their sight there was a shield of solid gold, forged from the sunlight. It was the Shield of Human Kindness that it is said no evil can penetrate, and it was passed to Burt. This was the treasure he needed to protect him.

The bubble floated down to Wood-Land, where it burst and they hopped out. They were both spellbound and breathless, and they rested on the shield's golden perch. Then Starling looked at Burt.

'Give us another kiss.'

Burt thought he owed her a big thank you so he closed his eyes and gave her a peck on the beak. Only it wasn't a beak, it was a pair of lips and Burt opened his eyes.

Yuk! He was kissing a girl.

'Hello,' she laughed. 'Don't be afraid.'

'I'm not afraid of anything. Who are you?'

'I'm Starling, your darling, and you came to rescue me.'

'No way, you're a girl. A real, live girl.'

'Well, duh.'

Burt felt foolish. He hadn't been expecting this at all. She was very pretty, with brown hair and green eyes and a little button nose. But she had a tattered old dress on that looked like it was made from a sack and her hair was all scruffy and tangled in knots. She wasn't at all like any girl Burt had ever seen.

'Um, I've been waiting for you for such a long time. There's something I want to show you, but we need to wait for the stars to come out.'

16

Starlight

They set up camp to wait until dark and collected wood for a fire. Burt lit the fire mainly to show off that he could and they sat on a log side by side. Then, because he was a bit embarrassed and his stomach was grumbling, he rooted around in his bag for some food. There wasn't much left from the fisherman's hut but there was something he had been saving up. It was a bag of marsh-mallows.

'Um, I've been saving these for a treat. Would you like some? We can toast some on the fire. You put them on sticks like this ...'

Burt picked up a twig and put a marshmallow on it. Then he held it over the flame until it was brown and bubbling and passed it to Starling. It had been a long time since she'd eaten any sweets and the present made her very happy.

Burt had got over the shock of Starling being a girl now and he asked her all about her life. When Starling was younger she had lost her family in a car crash and had been sent to her grandparents' farm. That was where she had first learned that she could speak to animals and the farm animals were her friends. Then one day she'd found a young badger caught in a trap and she had helped it to escape.

The badger was very grateful and very excited to find a human child that could speak the language of animals. He said no one else could do that, which made her feel special. She brought the badger food and tended to its wounds and when it had got better he'd asked her to visit his homeland.

Well, as you might have guessed this young badger was the same badger who was now emissary of Wood-Land. But this was several years ago now, which is a long time in animal years, and back then an old deer had been the emissary. She was a master of old wives' tales – the gossip passed on from the dawn of time – and she'd heard of something called the Prophecy of the Forgotten World.

'Have you heard the prophecy?' Starling asked.

'Yes, Badger told me something about Golden Children,' Burt said.

'That's us, Burt. The old deer taught me all of this and told me to stay with Badger until I saw a sign. Then one night when I was alone a star in the sky spoke to me. It said: *Starling, you are a Golden Child. Follow me to the lake and learn your fate.* Well, I followed my star – the brightest star in the sky – and it led me to a lake that was drenched in starlight. There was nobody there so I jumped in and swam. And I didn't notice at first that I'd turned into a frog.'

128

Burt remembered the frog kissing him and teaching him to swim, and she laughed.

'Yeah, I've been watching over you and giving you a hand. Anyway, the starlight seemed to rise up from the lake and I saw my dead parents take shape before me. They said I was special and called me Golden Girl and they told me to look for the other half of my soul because that would unlock the secrets that were held in my heart.

'I later found I could take three forms: a frog in the water, a bird in the sky and a river rat under the ground.

'The river rat was you!'

'Sorry if I sounded weird,' she said, laughing. 'I was just throwing you off the scent because you're so clever.'

Burt smiled.

'Anyway, I told Badger what my parents had said and he told me it meant that I had to find you in order to grow. So we're supposed to grow up now and return the world to its natural state, to the time when people lived in harmony with Mother Earth. I'm not sure how though.'

'When did you turn into a bird?'

'When I found my tree. It's the heart-shaped one you climbed to find me.'

'Wow, that's not even in Wood-Land.'

'It's not far if you can fly or swim.'

'Were the eggs in that nest yours?' Burt asked.

'No, I was just babysitting for a friend. I'm too young and well … human to lay eggs!' she added with a laugh.

'Well, you didn't do a very good job looking after them, flying off like that.'

'Er, excuse me, I told you to keep an eye on them before I left actually. I knew deep down you'd understand. That was my test to check you were the right boy for the job.'

'I didn't know how to speak bird, though.'

'You did, that's how you warned us about the fairy. Sometimes you don't know what you know.'

'Eh? Aw don't you start.'

'It's true.'

'OK, answer me this, clever-clogs. How come you can only turn into little animals? I want to turn into a lion.'

'Badger says it's because I'm cursed by the evil of man until we set Wood-Land free. I can't grow up as long as the Wood-Land is owned by man, you see? So I'm trapped in these limited forms, unable to fulfil my destiny.'

'What's destiny?'

'It's what you're going to be when you grow up. Badger says ours is written in the stars. He says their patterns tell a story like a secret language, and they led me to the Lake of Prophecy. That's where I was told I would know the other half of my soul as a reflection of myself; and I saw you in the lake when you made your wishes in the well. Your fate has put you to the test. You had to learn to tunnel, swim and fly like me and to fight the evil and set me free. That's why I gave you a helping hand,' she said with a wink.

'As if I needed a helping hand!' Burt said, a little irked.

'Everyone does,' she reassured him, though he looked unconvinced.

'Anyway,' she soon went on, 'they said the Golden Boy would be a daydreamer and a know-it-all and he would fight evil with the heart of a lion, and you're everything I expected you to be. I'm not disappointed at all.'

Burt gulped and went red but she wouldn't shut up and kept looking at him.

'And when you have triumphed over your demons and set the Wood-Land free we can be anything that we want to be. Together we can save the world!'

'What do I have to do?' Burt said uncertainly.

'Just follow your heart.'

'Yeah, but what does that actually mean?'

'It means you have to do what I tell you to do.'

'Oh, OK,' Burt said sheepishly.

'Tonight we will travel by starlight to the lake where it all began and there we will forge our diamond-coated armour. All of your tasks are now done except one; we must defeat the monster and then I think we'll grow up.'

Burt was relieved the tests were over and relaxed. 'My tree Buddy said not to grow up too quickly. There's plenty of time, and my dad always says you shouldn't wish your life away. I'd like to go back to being a little boy again after all this.'

Starling thought carefully about this. When the

stars came out she looked up and read them like a map.

'It's this way. Follow me.'

Everywhere you looked you could see a star. It was like the sky was full of tiny suns, and Burt wondered whether they had planets with people on looking back at him.

When they arrived at their destination the lake was bathed in starlight. It glittered on the ripples like diamonds raining down from the heavens.

'Now we have to swim, but we must keep our human form.' They jumped in fully clothed and swam together and the starlight twinkled around their shoulders. It seemed to follow them and collect up around them like a magical bubble bath. By the time they got out they were covered from head to toe in starlight.

'Now we have to seal it with a kiss.'

'Do your plans always involve this much kissing?' Burt complained.

'Just do as you're told.'

As they kissed, the starlight bound and their armour took shape. Beautiful diamond-clad suits formed around them and helmets covered their heads; and it all glistened with a fabulous nightlight that made it look like a force field.

'This is the Armour of Love. Neither of us can be harmed while the other is safe, so to get us the baddies would have to strike us both down at once. Now we will always know evil because evil fears love and thrives in its absence.

'Wow, I think I can see in the dark now.'

'Yeah, me too. The visor of the helmet seems to light up the whole world.'

'I wish I'd had this before. I was scared of the dark and I kept getting lost. ... Starling?'

'Yes?'

'I had a dream once about a girl who was saying something underwater. I couldn't remember it very well but I couldn't forget it either. It was a bit like tonight and she looked a bit like you, but ... how come?'

'That must have come from the wishing well. Just as I dreamed of you, you dreamed of me, too. Sometimes your dreams tell you what's happening in the waking world and they give you signs to see you through.'

'Yeah, I know. You should always follow your dreams, I think.'

'Ahem,' said an embarrassed voice. 'Captain Firebrand reporting for duty, Sir! I have come to guide you to the mountains and to give you tidings of war. Erm, oh, how rude of me, this is Dilly and Dally our cavalry deer. They run swiftly to danger and can spear baddies with their antlers. Dilly is your steed, Sir Burt, and I will ride with you. Dally will carry Starling and my lovely wife Dawn, whom you've met. ... Anyway, what were you two lovebirds doing?'

'Shut up!' Starling complained.

'Thank you, Captain,' Burt said, trying not to blush. 'Let's go at once. We can talk on the way.'

17

Preparing for Battle

They rode through the night like shooting stars with Dilly and Dally bounding swiftly through the trees as if they were fleeing danger, not running towards it.

Burt's heart went out to Sandy. He wished she knew he was coming and he hoped and prayed that she was safe; but Starling kept him distracted by keeping him talking. He felt as if he'd known her for his entire life.

'Riding a deer isn't very comfortable, is it?' he observed, rubbing his bottom as he did so.

'You have to try and relax your muscles so that you move with it. Otherwise you're in for a rough ride.'

'Can't we fly instead? You could navigate by the stars.'

'We could transform and our armour would change to match our shape, but you would have to leave your sword and shield with Firebrand. It's too heavy for us to take to the skies.'

Firebrand was a bit upset by Burt's suggestion. 'We are your escort, Sir Burt. I'm afraid I must insist you stay with us until we rendezvous with our forces.'

'Who are the enemy again? I mean, I know Hades.'

The dark forces of mankind do not take human form as a rule. Ghosts, fairies, goblins, trolls, witches and wizards ... you name it. They want to control Wood-Land because, like us, they have precious little space to live.'

They start out as people, but once they turn bad they cannot show themselves to the adult world. While we animals can flee, if an adult human sees them they are done for. So they go underground or flee to the hills and find a hiding place; but what they really want is to take Wood-Land from the animal kingdom and use it for their evil ends.

'So how can they fight with Hades? He looks like a man, so they'd just turn to stone if he saw them.'

'That he can take human form is a sign of his power. He is their king, the Lord of the Underworld, but you may find he looks different when you see him next. His evil is growing.'

'And what about Sandy? Where is she being kept?' Starling asked kindly because she knew how worried Burt was.

'She will be with the other captives up in the caves,' Dawn replied. 'He keeps all the children he captures up there.'

'What will we do with all of them?' Starling asked.

'We'll turn them into warriors like us. The enemy won't know what's hit them,' Burt replied.

136

Not all children are like us, Burt. Be sure you don't ask too much of them; they will be terribly afraid.'

The only thing to be afraid of is of being afraid because the only way the monsters can get you is if you let them. I can teach them how to fight. I think that's my destiny.'

Starling looked at him dreamily; she was very impressed by this.

They came to the border of Wood-Land which ran along the crest of a hill and beneath them was a sight to behold. A mountain that looked like it had been chopped in half filled their view. And beneath the wall of jagged rock there were enough animals to fill a playground, all hustling and bustling about. Almost every grown-up animal in Wood-Land had travelled here to help in any way they could. They stood in their tribes and Burt could just make out Badger standing on a rock and talking to them.

Firebrand hopped down and spoke. 'It seems Badger has successfully mustered the troops. Let me brief you on my battle plan.'

'Sir Burt, he began, 'let this be your first lesson in warfare. If you have to fight, you must play to your strengths and every animal has different strengths. Let me explain. The enemy will march in a set formation with their strongest forces in the centre of the battlefield. We animals are less powerful than the forces massed against us, so we must play to our strengths. We will use our speed and our movement to confuse and outmanoeuvre the enemy, causing them to lose discipline and break ranks. Only then will we send in our heavy troops to engage them one on one, honing in on them as a predator hunts its prey.'

'Have you ever played football, Burt?' Dawn could see Burt was getting confused. 'It's a bit like a game of football ...'

Burt nodded excitedly. Starling tutted and went off in search of Badger.

'Yes, that's exactly right,' Firebrand continued. 'We will use your fastest troops on the flanks to run behind the enemy lines, sending their defences into disarray. That's where the deer come in, led by Dilly and Dally here.'

'Yeah and when we get there, we'll charge them up the backside with our antlers and force them forward towards the forest,' Dally said. The deer were both grinning manically as though they couldn't wait for the call to arms.

'The next fastest and the most manoeuvrable of our troops are none other than us foxes,' Firebrand went on. 'A short sharp spear is our weapon of choice, which we can use to throw or smite the enemy like a thorn in its side.'

'Yes, but our main task is to sow confusion in the enemy's ranks, finding the gaps in their defences,' Dawn interrupted.

Yes,' Firebrand said, 'we'll attack first, then withdraw, then counterattack with the cavalry when they charge. Then it will be the badgers' turn. They are our heavy infantry. They are stocky and sturdy, and let me tell you, with a

club in its hand a badger is a match for anyone.'

'I see you're talking about my people.' Badger
had walked up the hill towards them hand in hand
with Starling.

'Fine fighters we are, though we avoid it if we
can ... The troops are assembled and have been
briefed on your battle plan, Captain Firebrand.
The scouts and special forces have also been
dispatched.'

'Excellent work, Badger. And the air force?'

'Ready and waiting; they're concealed in the
trees so the enemy don't suspect our strength.'

'What are ... all the things you just said?' Burt
asked. He felt as though he should know who he
was fighting with. He was also impatient to find
out who the enemy was.

'We've sent the smaller birds and the rabbits to
spy and scout out the enemy positions. They will
let us know what we're up against. The special
forces are one of our secret weapons. They are
mostly made up of the rats and ferrets and other
martial arts experts from the forest. We call them
the shadow fighters. They'll sneak up on the
enemy and take out any stragglers, particularly
the troublesome ghosts they use for spying.

'And the air force are ...?'

'Ah yes, our friends from the trees,' Badger said.
'We have Starling to thank for that one.'

Starling blushed and told Burt about the birds
of prey. The falcons and hawks have come; they
will attack any witches and wizards that take

139

flight. You have to watch out for witches and wizards, Burt; they shower fireworks down on our troops, which can be very dangerous. Then there are the eagles. They soar high above the enemy just as the squirrels are firing acorn bombs, then they swoop down and ... what's so funny?'

Burt thought that sounded hilarious. 'What can a squirrel do?'

'You've clearly never been hit by an acorn bomb,' said Firebrand. 'They fly like bullets from a gun, and when they're out of ammo, they become paratroopers, thrown by the eagles right into the enemy's faces. Yes, squirrels are the most fearsome fighters of all. You have to have more guts than brains to be a flyboy.'

'But I've seen squirrels running away all the time.'

'Running into the trees, I would wager. Squirrels are the sworn protectors of the trees. They follow the trees' orders in return for food and shelter.'

'So you see all the animals in Wood-Land have an important task here. We are too few to waste talents,' Dawn said. She seemed a bit annoyed Burt had laughed. 'Even the mice – they tend to our wounded and stockpile ammunition for the squirrels.'

'Don't forget the trick we have up our sleeves,' Starling said, smiling.

'Ah yes, our buddies the trees are the heavy artillery. If we can draw the enemy close enough, the trees will throw stones into the enemy's ranks like catapults.'

Burt thought this sounded cool and smiled. Starling, however, told him sharply that war wasn't a game. It was deadly serious and no smiling matter. 'Boys!' she said.

A bunny rabbit hopped into view, saluted and then collapsed in a heap. Badger bounded over to it and it whispered its news in his sensitive ears.

'It's as we feared. The main body of their forces are mountain trolls.'

'Oh no!' Dawn cried. 'If we lose, they'll clear Wood-Land.'

'If we lose, Wood-Land is doomed anyway. They'll cut down the wild trees and turn it all to undergrowth. Mountain trolls are close cousins of river trolls; they hide in the hills and blend into rocks and they carry metal axes.'

'There're goblins as well,' Badger continued sadly. 'Missile troops with bows and arrows. But Starling's right, the witches and wizards and their blasted fireworks are the worst.'

'And then there's the fact that we're outnumbered two to one,' Badger said. 'The scout says they're six hundred strong at least. Go on, Captain Firebrand, you must address your troops. They'll need all of the courage they can get. And tell them to fall back to this hill on Wood-Land's edge. The enemy are almost upon us and they're like sitting ducks beneath that cliff.'

'Would you like me to talk to them?' Burt asked.

'Ordinarily we would but we have a secret mission for you and Starling. There is the matter of this monster of yours, Hades, and his captives.

141

He commands these forces; they fight because he tells them to. If you can cut off his head, you will cut off the head of the whole army, then you'll need to lead the children back down the mountain pass. If any of them are fit to fight, we may need their help, but we'll do our best to break the evil forces ourselves.'

'Just wait until these monsters meet my friend Sandy,' Burt said.

'I'll call my bird friends. There'll know where Hades is hiding,' Starling said helpfully.

You must travel deep into enemy territory and take him out. Then return if you can and help our forces finish off the enemy. You will have to travel on foot, I'm afraid. So please set off immediately and hurry! We are counting on your safe return.'

'That sounds like a plan,' Burt said.

18

How to Fight Monsters and Win

They set off immediately and the birds carried news to them on the wind. The monster was up a mountain pass beyond the cliff face. He lay in wait beside a complex of caves, guarding the children within and relaying orders for the battle ahead.

'He stays there with his victims because he draws strength from their fears,' one bird told them. 'It feeds his evil. You will not recognise him from before.'

Apparently the fisherman had been busy since he'd lost Burt and his dog Wolf. He had raided the nearby town and had taken all of the children there hostage, including Burt's school friends.

'What kind of monster hunts children? I dread to think what he's done with them,' said Starling.

'I wonder what he looks like now? He keeps on changing,' said Burt.

'Badger says he captures and corrupts the innocent because their fears feed the evil in the Underworld, where he claims lordship. He holds power over the dead and the damned, and he will only grow stronger if we don't stop him now.'

They reached a rocky outcrop and peeked over. There ahead was a huge hole in the cliff face, with jagged edges like the fangs of a snake poking out from the top. And there beside it, sitting on a great stone column like a stool, was a giant. He had an awful pointy face like Flutterby's and huge big ears the size of satellite dishes. His eyes were staring intently – he was counting his troops as they marched to war beneath him. It was Hades the fisherman all right, but he had grown to a terrible size.

A witch flew up to take her orders, then she left to deliver his plan of attack. He sat there mulling something over and picking his teeth with a huge stick.

Hades still looked like the fisherman and wore the same clothes, only everything had grown. He had wellington boots on the size of Burt, jeans, a belt and a blue coat without arms, revealing his big muscles and white skin. Burt was working himself up, and just as he was about to step out and charge him, Starling grabbed his hand.

'Don't be stupid, Burt. We have to be clever about this and play to our strengths. A head-on attack is just what he wants.'

'Well, what do you suggest?'

'We sneak past him unnoticed and get to the children first. Then they can help us in our fight.'

'He's going to notice us going past him even if we flew in.'

'I have a trick up my sleeve. It's called dream-whispering. I think I can send him to sleep. Don't move a muscle – I'll be right back.'

With that Starling transformed into a bird and flew off. She seemed to be flying away from the cave at first, but actually she was being clever and flying far enough around so that the giant wouldn't notice her coming up behind him. The only problem was he was sitting close to the cliff face, so there wasn't much space to sneak up in. Starling circled above the giant's head and then did something incredibly daring: she swooped down, pulled up at the last moment, and then perched expertly on a rock, close to the giant's big ears.

She did all of this without a sound and the giant didn't even blink. Burt's heart was in his mouth. It was even scarier watching someone he cared about in danger than being in danger himself. If the giant noticed Starling, she wouldn't be able to escape. She was within his grasp, though she acted as if this didn't matter one jot. She obviously had a plan.

Burt was cursing himself. He shouldn't have let her take such a risk. Then he heard Starling begin to sing ever so softly and he thought she was a goner for sure.

Incredibly though the giant didn't spin around and biff her; instead, he started to drop off to sleep. When he had started to snore, it sounded like a thunderstorm. But Starling just hopped forward on to his shoulder and sang louder. Burt approached now in little boy form and heard what Starling was singing about:

Fisherman of the Enchanted River
Hunter of the wild
Woodsman of the natural world
You will hear this Golden Child.

Be you man or monster
You will hear the children's cries
Let their fears take you over
And show your evil through their eyes.

Hades of the Underworld,
Do you think your time has come?
Do you think the love you lack is lost?
Well, we've come to prove you wrong.

There is one here who is heaven sent
And he comes to conquer your attack
There is one here who has seen your hell
And has come to send you back!

The one who got away has come
You have feared him from the start.
Would you like to know your nightmare's name?
It is brave Sir Burt the Lion Heart!

With that the giant started to wriggle and squirm and talk in his sleep as if he had some horrible disease. Starling turned into a girl again and smiled at Burt.

'That's dream-whispering,' she said.

'That'll teach him,' was all Burt could think to say. He felt a bit mushy after hearing that.

'C'mon, let's go and find the others, quick.'

Starling took him by the hand and led him into the cave.

The cave was deep and dark but their armour lit the way. Burt kept his shield and sword at the ready and tried to keep up with Starling as she darted this way and that. He was determined to keep her safe.

Starling stopped suddenly and Burt almost bumped into her. It was a good job he didn't because blocking their path was a huge pit that drilled through the mountain and fell away into the bowels of the Earth. Burt guessed it went all the way down into the Underworld.

Hades had been clever. He hadn't tried to lock the children up. Locks can be opened. Instead he had reached across the gap and placed the children one by one on a ledge on the other side, with no escape but down.

'Ten, twenty, thirty – there must be a hundred children there.'

Burt looked around desperately.

'Sandy!'

Woof! Sandy sounded delighted. 'Oh Burt, I never thought I'd see you again. I'm so glad that you're safe. But what are you doing here? Has that awful giant gone?'

'No,' Burt said. 'Sandy, how are you? Are the children OK?'

The children were all huddled together. He was going to shout across to reassure the others, who looked so frightened and confused that they couldn't speak, but Starling grabbed his arm.

'No, the awful giant hasn't gone, so maybe you should shut up so that you don't wake him up!'

Unfortunately, it was too late.

'Uh, eh, oh.'

The giant coughed and leapt up outside and the ground seemed to shudder like an earthquake.

'WHAT'S ALL THAT RACKET IN THERE? I THOUGHT I TOLD YOU LOT TO SHUT UP! PERHAPS I SHOULD THROW YOU DOWN THE PIT OF ETERNAL DAMNATION RIGHT NOW INSTEAD. EH?! DID YOU HEAR WHAT I SAID? THEN MAYBE I'D GET SOME PEACE.'

For a moment there was silence, then great booming footsteps started to make their way towards them.

'Oh no, we haven't got long.'

Starling transformed into a bird and flew over to the ledge. She tried to console all the children there but she didn't know what to do; she couldn't very well pick them up and fly them across when she was just a little bird. And there was no way they could jump the gap, even if they had been in a fit state. What they needed was a bridge, but there was nothing to use. The cave was bare.

'Starling, we have to get out of here.'

'No, I'm not leaving them.'

'Please don't go,' one of the children said. 'He said he was going to throw us into that pit and leave us underground when the battle is won.'

'He hasn't won yet!' Starling said.

'I'm scared of heights. Please get us out of here!' another stammered.

The footsteps were almost upon them now. It was too late to leave anyway. So Burt turned and ran to face his foe.

'Stay there and protect the children, Starling. Remember my armour will protect me as long as you're safe.'

Burt felt his armour glow brighter and brighter. It was telling him that the evil was close.

Then he turned a corner and saw the giant stooped down low and struggling down the tunnel. Burt had wanted to face him outside but this was much better. There was plenty of space for him to move around because he was small and quick, but the giant could barely move at all.

Burt opened his visor to show his face.

'Hello, Hades, did you have a nice sleep?'

As his eyes fell on Burt, a look of recognition, then of horror, fell across his face. He had just dreamed that this boy had thrown him into the pit of eternal damnation. But how could he? He was so small.

The giant shrugged off his fears and gave Burt a terrible leer.

'I have some unfinished business with you. You went and killed my dog, didn't you? I kept yours alive just long enough to draw you here. Now I'll kill her, then you. I'm going to crunch your nasty little fish bones and turn your flesh into tomato paste.'

'Hades, I'm wearing magic armour. Sticks and stones can't break my bones, and your threats certainly don't hurt me.'

'Well, let's see about that. He flicked the stick he'd been using to pick his teeth at Burt and it flew through the air like a dagger. Burt didn't even try to dodge it. He just closed his helmet visor and it bounced off harmlessly.

'Ooohh, that makes things interesting. Let's try this.'

The giant tore into the wall of the cave and the rock crumbled and came off in his hands like lumps of dry clay. Then it threw the rocks at Burt, who ducked and dived and blocked them with his shield. One got through and hit him on the head, and although his magic helmet protected him the force of the blow knocked him back into the wall.

'Do you really think you stand a chance against

the might of Hades? I am as old as the hills and as big as the trees.'

'Then why do you pick on people younger and smaller than you, you big bully?'

'Yes well, now I'm picking on you, aren't I, you little runt. What are you gonna do about it?'

'I'm going to put you in your place.'

Burt charged forward and Hades leant forward to grab him. But at the last moment Burt skidded down on his bum and shot between his legs. Then before the giant could turn he jumped and slashed him behind the knee. His great fat leg buckled and he screamed, then he pivoted on his knee and stared at Burt with big cross-eyes.

Hades roared and Burt saw the horrible animal teeth and pitch-black tongue he'd seen in the Underworld. His mind clearly hadn't been playing tricks. It was preparing him for what was to come.

'We told you what happened to little boys who went to the woods on their own. We told you what happened to little boys who didn't do as they're told. You might escape me once, little boy; you might even escape me twice but not for ever. There is nowhere to run and nowhere to hide that I can't find. I swear I won't let you go again. I am your comeuppance and this mountain is your tomb. This mountain will swallow you whole.'

'Go back to the Underworld where you belong.'

'The bell tolls for you, Burt Marshmallow.'

'And I think you've got too big for your wellington boots, giant. And you might want to think about brushing your teeth more often.'

Burt had the strangest feeling. He felt weird. Using the power of his mind he found he could read the giant's feelings, and they warned him what he was going to do next. If he was going to punch or kick, a little alarm went off in Burt's mind, and he just avoided it. The giant banged one mighty fist down and then another again and again, but Burt ducked and weaved and jumped out of the way and he was always one step ahead of Hades.

As he grew in confidence, he started slashing at the giant's grasping hands and stabbing at his feet. Slowly but surely Hades was getting worn down. Burt was actually winning and he was pushing the giant back towards the underground pit.

Then Burt had an idea. He let himself get a little too close so that he was within the giant's grasp. He was using himself as bait again …

'What does it feel like to be beaten up by a little boy,' Burt asked. He expected Hades to lash out but he didn't.

'I'm going to show you what happens to little boys who don't do as they're told.'

Hades leant back and in one movement he pulled his big leather belt from his trousers and lashed out at Burt, using it like a whip.

'Burt, watch out!' Starling cried out.

Burt leapt in the air but was knocked off his feet.

'Ooohh, is that your girlfriend? I wonder what would happen if I threw her into the pit of eternal damnation, along with that dog of yours.'

'You'll have to kill me first.'

'That can be arranged. I'm going to bounce you like a basketball, you incy-wincy little squirt.'

'I have more than magic armour, Hades! This is the Shield of Human Kindness, which your evil cannot penetrate.'

Hades slammed his fist down but Burt blocked the blow. Hades shrieked with pain as his hand clattered into the shield and crumpled up. Then, to everyone's surprise including Burt's, the shield sprang to life. The sunlight it stored burst forth from its face and it shone like a laser into Hades' eyes. He lifted his arm to block it out but he was too late. Hades was now blind.

'Aaarrrrggghhh, my eyes. I can't see. I can't see. Where are you? Where are you? What have you done to me?'

Hades began thrashing around and banging into the walls. Then he calmed down and started sniffing and listening, because he still had his giant ears and a quite gigantic nose.

'Never mind, I can always sniff out a little boy. Let's see, you're this way, and all the other nasty little monsters are behind me.'

'Hades,' Burt called as he approached him. 'This is the Sword of Justice. You might not be able to see it but I promise you you'll feel it. By its authority I command you to return to the Underworld, never to return. You can go into that pit with your head or without it.'

'I think I'll save you for last so you can watch me kill your friends one by one. Even without my sight

154

I am infinitely more powerful than you,' the giant boomed.

Hades bent down towards Burt and roared like thunder and he swung his leather whip again, but Burt was prepared. He jumped into the air and spun like a helicopter with his sword outstretched and he chopped off the giant's big black tongue, as it poked out of his open mouth.

He landed in a crouch, and the tongue flopped down in front of him like a giant slug covered in slime.

'Try telling me what to do now, giant. You should learn to watch your mouth next time.'

Hades shrieked like a wounded animal and began raging and tearing and banging at the rock. The ceiling above Burt's head crumbled and caved in and he held up his shield just in time.

Now Burt was trapped. He struggled to free himself as Hades ran forward and kicked him like a football, slamming him against a wall.

'Ow!' Burt staggered up to his feet dizzily. Then as he came to he heard an awful shriek and a yelp. He looked up and to his horror he saw the giant was standing on the other ledge holding Starling in one hand and Sandy in the other. He was dangling them over the abyss and laughing.

'DWOP YAW SWORD AND SHIELD OR I'LL DWOP EM OTH!' the giant managed.

'OK, OK, please don't.' Burt did as he was told. What choice did he have?

'OK, OW ICH ON YOU WANNA KEEP? SHUD

155

I OO A DIP? I INK I'LL DWOP YOUR DOG TO GET OO BACK FOR MY OLF!'

Oh no. Burt couldn't choose between them. How could he? But Starling gave him the answer in birdsong.

'Burt, stop being stupid. If he drops me, I'll just fly free.'

'Oh yeah he said to himself relieved. Please, Mr, just don't drop my dog.'

'OH WELL ICKLE GIRL. I GUESS OR BOYFRIEND DOESN'T IKE YOU.'

'Oh shut up, you big bumbling buffoon.'

The giant dropped her but she immediately turned into a bird and started swooping about and pecking at his eyes. He dropped Sandy but she managed to cling on to the ledge and he swiped blindly at Starling. He caught her with a clumsy blow, and Burt heard Starling scream and collapse.

The sound of her scream echoing around did something strange to Burt. It was as if the fire that burned in his soul had suddenly spread to every nerve in his body before firing out of his glaring eyes. He pounced and bounded forward into a run, full of a terrible determination to destroy the giant or die trying, and he didn't even notice that he had turned into a lion.

He ran forward roaring with all the might in the world and leapt across the great pit, clearing it with ease, then pounded into the giant's chest and clung on with his claws. The giant's head slammed back against the rock wall behind, and Burt

156

continued to maul him. The giant was up in a flash but he was done for. He wavered and fell towards the pit like a tree that had been chopped down. Such was his size that he didn't fall down the hole; he fell across it and bridged the gap.

Burt transformed back into a boy and looked around for Starling and Sandy. Sandy jumped up and licked his face; then she barked and herded the children into a line. They filed across to the other side of the abyss as the giant clung on for dear life, helpless to stop them. All Burt could think about was finding Starling. Then he saw her pretty little face lying against the wall. She was lying completely still but her eyes were wide open and she was staring at him.

'Quick, get up before Hades recovers again! Get up, Starling. What are you staring at? Why are you just lying there?'

'Because I'm flabbergasted, you nincompoop!' Starling couldn't believe what she'd just seen. Burt had really turned into a lion. 'How did you do that?'

The cave started to crumble and boulders fell all around them. They were running across the giant's body when a rock caught it with a glancing blow, making Hades wince and swing, so that now he had to cling to the side with his hands alone. They had just got across in time, but the giant was pulling himself up even as they stepped off. A great hand came out and tripped Burt with its fingertips as he ran away.

'Keep going, Starling,' Burt shouted as he spun around.

The giant was just clambering up on to the ledge ready to attack again when Burt saw a glint out of the corner of his eye.

He picked up his sword and charged forward, then spinning in mid-air he chopped the giant's head clean off.

'Don't say I didn't warn you.'

The giant's expression was frozen in a puzzled grimace. Its head slipped off his shoulders and tumbled towards Burt like a boulder. He leapt backwards as the giant's body slipped and fell into the abyss and the head flopped down on its side and turned to stone in front of his eyes. The head of Hades might still be found in the same spot to this day – if only you could get into the cave!

Burt hurriedly picked up his shield and ran outside, dodging boulders as the cave collapsed around him.

Then he caught up with Starling and the others and they ran as fast as their legs could carry them until they came to the cliff edge. There they stopped, bent double and wheezing. Then Burt, Starling and Sandy started checking over everyone.

Beneath them a battle raged. When he got a chance, Burt looked to see what was happening. He was shocked to see the animals were losing. He knew what needed to be done.

The animals were outnumbered and outgunned. Witches and wizards were firing sparklers and bangers and rockets in all directions. Badgers clubbed at mountain trolls, and they swung back with their terrible axes. The foxes, mounted on their deer comrades, charged recklessly into the enemy ranks, spreading mayhem among their own ranks at least as much as the enemy's. The eagle bombers seemed to have run out of ammunition and were dive-bombing the goblin archers and throwing suicidal squirrels from their talons in an effort to stop the arrows raining down on the good guys.

The animals seemed to be falling further and further back towards the woods. Then, without warning, they turned tail and ran away!

The evil army let out an almighty cheer and charged for the trees with their axes at the ready. But then, as they got to within a stone's throw of Wood-Land's border, something threw a colossal stone, which tore through the enemy army like a bowling ball. Then a hailstorm of stones flew from the forest, clattering into the baddies and sending them scattering like skittles. Witches were knocked off their broomsticks and exploded in a fountain of flames; mountain trolls were crushed like trodden-on toads. Then Burt saw that the animals had regrouped in their units and were preparing to counterattack.

He turned to the children who stared awestruck at the battle scene. It looked like the trees had evened things up but there was still a fight to be had.

'Boys and girls,' Burt began. 'I know you have just had your first experience of a monster and it was one of the worst experiences imaginable, but you have survived it unharmed. I know that you want to go home and forget that any of this happened but you can't – the monsters are here to stay, unless we fight back.

'I know you are afraid and that is a horrible feeling, but the best way to stop feeling afraid is to be brave and stand up for yourself! So an army of monsters stands in our way. We have an army on our side as well. The creatures of Wood-Land are fighting bravely for the right to live wild and free and I for one am going to fight with them. And if we all stick together, I'm sure that we'll win. So who's with me?'

At first no one spoke. Then one of Burt's friends from school stepped forward.

'We're in this battle now whether we like it or not. And if I had to pick the side that will win, even if it was *only* him, I would side with Burt. Did you see the way he beat up that giant!'

'For Burt the Lion Heart!' Starling shouted.

'For Burt the Lion Heart!' all the children cried in unison.

Woof, woof! Sandy added.

'OK, let's go and biff some baddies!'

With that, they all charged down the mountain pass and on towards the battle.

19

The End, Almost

They got to the bottom of the cliff and the baddies
were fighting at the top of the hill, near the trees.
Lots of weapons had been abandoned by fallen foes
and Burt had an idea. The children all dressed up
as trolls and goblins, taking the weapons and
clothes from bodies on the ground, then they snuck
up behind the remaining baddies.

'Keep fighting! Hades is sending reinforcements
from the hills,' cried a witch when she spotted
them. It was the witch they had seen talking to
Hades. She was leading the troops on the
battlefield.

Burt called to the witch and she came near.

'Hades said to give you something.' He was
wearing a troll tunic and helmet over his armour.

'Why's he giving you the orders? I'm his second-
in-command. Who are you?'

Burt gestured for her to come closer still
then, when she leant in, he cut her clean in
half.

'OK, everyone, show them you're not frightened.
Show them they messed with the wrong bunch of

kids. ... Charge!' Burt shouted, and the children roared as one.

The evil forces didn't know what had hit them. They were trapped between the animals and the children like the meat in a sandwich and they were quickly gobbled up.

Sandy was particularly ferocious and it wasn't long before the enemy troops all gave up because they were leaderless and surrounded. Only the witches and wizards flying overhead posed a problem.

But Firebrand hadn't lied about the squirrels. They were leaping from their eagle mounts on to witches' broomsticks as if they were the branches of a tree, and everywhere the enemy were plummeting down to earth. Some of the squirrels had taken control of the broomsticks and were flying kamikaze-style into the baddies. It was like mid-air dodgems! Burt, meanwhile, used his shield to deflect the fireworks back into the air, and he gave Starling his catapult and she shot the witches out of the sky.

After about half an hour, the battle was finally won. All that was left was to tidy up all the mess and get everybody home.

Thankfully all of their friends were safe and sound, although many animals had been killed or wounded. Badger hadn't fought at all. He was far too old. He thanked them and told them they would be forever friends, but that they had to get all the children home and return to their own families as well.

'Starling, I think it's time you went back to your grandparents' farm. It has been far too long and you're only a child.'

'No, I want to stay with you. And what about Burt?'

'Ah, tell Burt where your grandparents live.'

'The farm's near a village called Winston.'

'Whoa, that's the village I walk Sandy to,' Burt said excitedly. 'Come back, Starling, please! I'll finally have someone to play with when I'm at home.'

'OK, OK, I do want to but it's just ... well, I thought when this was over I would grow up and so would Burt and we'd live in Wood-Land together. Wood-Land is my home and I don't want to leave Badger.'

'I will visit you and you me,' Badger said kindly. 'This is not the end of our adventures but the beginning, Starling. I'm quite sure Burt will see to that. And you will grow up together, but all in good time! You mustn't wish your life away. If you grow up too soon, you'll miss all the fun.'

So Burt, Starling and Sandy led the children back to the town, and then on to their homes. Then they set off together for the village and Burt's house.

Starling was nervous because she hadn't seen her grandparents for a long time and she didn't know what to say. Burt knew exactly how she felt. This was going to take a lot of explaining.

'I can't very well tell them I'm the child of Mother Earth and I was trapped in the wild until

163

I found the boy who would save Wood-Land from its foes.'

'If you're the child of Mother Earth, what does that make me again?'

'You're my knight in shining armour. You came to set me free.'

After they had delivered all of the children to the village safely, Burt asked Starling whether she would like to come back with him. He knew his parents would look after her and contact her grandparents to check everything was OK.

They arrived at Burt's house eventually and both of them were very nervous. How were they going to explain themselves? Then, as they entered the garden, Burt got the shock of his life.

A horse chestnut tree had grown from the conker he had planted. His wish at the wishing well had at last been granted.